Stripah Love

Library of Congress Cataloging-in-Publication Data
Morris, Stephen Hunter
Stripah Love
2005
ISBN: 0-9764520-0-6

Cover design and typography by Michael Potts using
CorelDraw, PhotoPaint, and Quark. The body font is
Garamond, and the chapter heading font is Georgia.

Stripah Love

by Stephen Hunter Morris

The Public Press

Randolph   Caspar

Recipes

Stripah Love

Acknowledgement

Accolades are hard to find for Jack Gartside. He has fished every square inch of Boston Harbor (including the islands), and he tied his first fly with Ted Williams. He catches more fish than anyone and has more fun doing it.

His self-published The Flyfisherman's Guide to Boston Harbor is beyond definitive. You can order it from him directly ($29.95 plus $3.50 shipping and handling) at 14 Beach Road, Winthrop, MA 02152.

The only thing more remarkable than Jack Gartside's knowledge of Boston Harbor and striped bass is his willingness to share it, which he does through books, presentations, classes, and his website (www.jackgartside.com). He taught me everything I know about striped bass and salt-water fly fishing, but I learned only a fraction of what he has to teach.

-- *Stephen Hunter Morris*

To Bob, Connie, and Gordie.

Hunters of eternal summer.

Part 1
These Days

Chapter 1 - Four-letter Words

This is a story about fish-big fish, little fish, schools of fish, allegorical fish, alliterative fuckin' fish, mythical fish, fiberglass fish (more alliteration), but, above all, fried fish. Fish, too, is a four-letter word.

And it is also a story about shit-good, shit, bad shit, family shit, fish shit, literal shit, frustrating shit, happy shit, sad shit, loose shit, heavy duty shit, meaningless shit, metaphorical shit. But not fried shit. Actually, it's about fried shit, too, but not literal fried shit.

Shit.

Sandy Beach's Fishing Forecast for April

No reports of any stripers anywhere in the harbor, although schoolies are plentiful on the south side of Long Island. A few intrepid herring have been seen in local rivers, but the onslaught is still ahead.

This is the time for the final pre-season checklist:

- ☐ *Waders, fully waterproofed?*
- ☐ *Flies, numerous, sharp and organized so that you can find them when you need them?*
- ☐ *Tide chart highlighted?*
- ☐ *Time off from work arranged with the boss?*
- ☐ *30" minimum size marked on fly rod?*

You're ready. Go out to the back yard and practice, because they're on their way, heading towards Provincetown and a hard left towards Boston Harbor.

-Sandy Beach, from *The Boston Globe*

A small sign above the doorway reads, "Welcome to the edge of civilization."

Cuzzin's Bait and Tackle stands discordantly on what is now the busy suburban corner of Ocean Avenue and Germantown Pike in Quincy, Massachusetts. Built as the home of Gordon's SeaFood by Seamus "Bull" Gordon in 1933, it purveyed many a fried clam, filleted mackerel, and swordfish steak before the proprietor closed his doors in 1966. He retained the commercially-zoned piece of property which became, in sequence, a beauty shop, an antique store, a realtor's office, another beauty shop, and a lawyer's office. No one, however, could fully eradicate its fishy ancestry, not a quite a stench, but a subtle musk of mudflats and brine. Now, it has accumulated five decades (or should it be "decayeds") of shabbiness.

In 1982 the squat building became home to Cuzzin's Bait & Tackle, a business owned and operated by Bull's son, Lewis, known ubiquitously around Quincy as "Cuzzin." During the holidays he sells Christmas trees from Vermont. He'll sharpen knives and scissors anytime. From October to April, this is a place for the neighborhood degenerates to hang out and get discreetly drunk. From April to October, however, this is the starting line for men (and, increasingly, women) who go to the sea in search of sport, food, adventure, and spiritual connection. It exists anonymously in a neighborhood that has forgotten its proximity to the Atlantic.

The cosmetics are non-existent, unless you count peeling paint. Signage ("Blood worms, $.25 each," "We have sand eels," "Frozen Pogies") is hand-scrawled by the proprietor. There is an ample, unpaved parking lot that holds only

Cuzzin's shopworn GMC pick-up. At the rear of the lot is a tangle of sumac trees that have grown because nothing else would. Beyond that is the salt marsh and eventually the sea.

The basic structure is sound and refuses to fall down. "She's built good," Bull would say. These days, none of the customers object to the whiff of fish and the sea.

On a sunny April day a man of middle age stands before Cuzzin's Bait & Tackle. The forsythia is in bloom and the world is rejoicing at its freedom from winter. White clouds scud overhead joyfully, oblivious to the incessant traffic.

And the feeling is mutual.

The man is paralyzed, as if he has stepped into wet concrete that has now hardened around his ankles. He wears custom-made Italian loafers that he proudly tells people cost him over $400. He does not look a likely candidate for the purchase of blood worms or sand eels.

Arthur Gordon, "Artie," "Art," and "A.G." just doesn't get it. At 52, of medium height, with well-coifed, but thinning gray hair, he has recently completed his eleventh, and perhaps, final movie. As the writer, director, and executive producer of *My Mother, My Lover, My Wife, and, now, My Sales Manager* he has laid one of the biggest bombs in Hollywood history. His sin? Political incorrectness in the first degree. He crossed the line and is paying the price. Single-handedly, he galvanized the feminists of America to bring their collective wrath upon his balding pate.

Now he stands, immobilized, before the rundown structure that launched an equally modest family legend. He has come home.

The Gordons came to Boston by way of Nova Scotia in the mid-1800s. By the turn of the century they were well established as accountants and actuaries and dentists in

Dorchester and South Boston and started coming to the Quincy shore for aquatic recreation. At first these were manly affairs, the men staying in simple camps that accommodated expeditions to hunt ducks, catch flounder, or dig clams. Bull and his three brothers, including Artie's father Bruce, weren't consciously aware of it, but they were continuing a tradition that had been lived by generations of Wompatuck Indians before. As the Gordon boys grew older, they began to bring their girl friends on their salty excursions. Their camps became gentrified, a great place to spend the Roaring 20s. Then, the girl friends became wives, and there were lots of little kids. Then the kids grew up and had kids of their own, including Artie and the little red head who everyone called Cuzzin.

There, two generations in a paragraph. Back up.

The Depression came. All jobs were lost. Just like that. The Depression was the Middle Ages for its generation. But it was also the darkness from which was seen the light at the end of the tunnel. We fought in the Big One, and afterwards everyone came home and was prosperous. The ones who were entrepreneurial became rich. Back up.

Bull started going to the local docks where the Portuguese fishermen of Hough's Neck worked out of small shacks. He couldn't afford to buy their fish, but he convinced them if they would consign him their catch, he could sell it in Boston for more than they could make wholesaling it themselves. It worked, and Gordon Sea Foods was born. Before long, the business needed a building to store and refrigerate the fish and shellfish, and Bull found the location at the corner of Ocean and Germantown.

But the best laid plans went awry as the 30s became the 40s, and with the passage of time the shallow waters of Quincy Bay became increasingly polluted. The delicious, sweet clams from the nearby mudflats required several days of purification before they could be consumed. With that much cost added in transportation and processing it became more desirable to buy clams from the open waters of Ipswich to the north. The Portuguese fishermen gave up and disappeared. Now Bull had to drive into Boston to the Fish Pier where the deep water boats docked.

Since he had a building containing fish and shellfish, Bull decided to sell some directly to the public, and since the people were going to eat them eventually, he might as well give them the option of immediate gratification by frying them on the premises.

Bull became pretty damn good at frying. "It's all in the grease" became his stock answer whenever asked how he managed to get such a dry, crisp crust without losing the tang of freshness in the flesh of haddock, cod, flounder, smelt (in the fall), clams, scallops, and shrimp. (For the record he also sold mackerel, pollock, striped bass, and the occasional swordfish or halibut if someone got lucky. He also fried potatoes and onion rings and served a cole slaw and tartar sauce that he made fresh each morning.)

Bull's fish and chips were the best in Boston. On Friday nights and summer weekends the line for take-out would spill around the corner. The few tables were jammed. The place sizzled. As Artie and, eventually, Cuzzin became teenagers they were pressed into service manning the fryers, listening to the grease, barking out orders so that the fried morsels from the sea could be consumed while they glistened with heat.

Artie's to do list for April
> Call Elaine for update
> Go to Boston, scope out cottage
> Go to London to receive award
> Fix up cottage
> Heal thyself

Sometimes he who hesitates is found, and so it was with Artie. The aluminum screen door of the bait shop flew open with a bang, and a man with shoulder-length gray hair, with a blue bandana around his forehead charged out carrying a sign "We Got Sea Worms!!" He wore a well-tattered flannel shirt that was unbuttoned, freeing his ample beer gut to greet the Spring. The sleeves of the shirt had been torn off, and his arms were covered in faded tattoos. His beard, or more precisely the gray hair that grew from his face, was long and undisciplined. There was not even a hint of red hair.

Initially, he paid no heed to the man on the sidewalk watching him. But as he grew exasperated at trying to attach his sign to some woefully insufficient nail stubs, he turned his irritation on the bystander.

"You got a fucking staring problem?" he asked.

Then came the moment of recognition.

Is this unique to the human species? Artie wondered later as he reflected back on his reunion with Cuzzin. *Years pass, faces change, hair falls out, kids are born, wives come and go, and yet it only takes one instant, one look in the eye, one syllable of speech for one member of the human species to recognize another with whom he is acquainted. You walk on the city street or through a mall or airport, and you see thousands of faces. The eyes scan them all. Nope, nope, nope, nope. They're all strangers. Until there's the moment. The click that occurs. Could this be captured on film? How could it be expressed? It wouldn't work. You'd need a two shot, reactions from both players. You'd need thirty seconds, maybe forty-five, to communicate what in real life takes a nanosecond.*

Cuzzin's moment of recognition, while joyous, was none too eloquent. "Ahhtee. You fuckin' gotta be kiddin'. You fuckin' gotta be kiddin' ME. I can't fuckin' believe it. Ahhtee. You fuckin' gotta be kiddin." And they embrace.

Inside, the men sit at stools by what used to be the ordering counter for the fish and chips. Cuzzin spews words: Jeez, Ahhtee, goodtaseeyuh! Howyabeen? What bringsyaback? Hey, jizwanna beer?

It's still morning.

Aww, fukkit, Ahhtee. You only go this way once. Beer tastes best in the morning.

Cuzzin cracked open a sixteen ounce can of Old Milwaukee and slid it to him. He already had a can open for himself.

Hirstoyou. To whateva brotcha home.

They clink cans.

There are no customers for bait this morning. A few regular degenerates stop by, looking to sneak in a quick beer with Cuzzin, but they are scared off by Artie's polished demeanor. It's a perfect time to catch up.

Bull Gordon, Cuzzin's father and Artie's uncle, never set foot in Scotland, but he put on a righteous brogue, drrrragging his "Rrrrs" and complaining fierrrcely about the wrongs heaped upon his people by the bloody British. He owned a kilt that was worn with great ceremony at the annual Fourth of July costume parade at Indian Mound. And he was thrifty.

It was through thrift that he found fortune.

No part of a fish was discarded. The bits of white flesh found their way into "Gordon's Own Seafood Chowder." The eyeballs, innards, and skeletons were ground into "Gordon's Own Miracle Fertilizer" which was stored in galvanized cans in back of the shop until the city came and made him take away the malodorous mess. (They did him a favor, because the stench was keeping away the fish & chips customers as well.)

The 40s became the 50s. The commercial fishing business died off, but the fried foods part of his business prospered.

The surrounding area was swelling with Irish refugees from South Boston and Italians from the city's North End. Both groups were heavily Catholic, and on Fridays a line would form starting around five o'clock for Bull's fried seafood, which everyone knew was the best around. For several frenzied hours Bull would be battering and frying fish, clams, scallops, potatoes, and onion rings as fast as his frothing fryers could handle them.

He became a virtuoso of the deep fat fryer. He knew the right consistency of the batter. His oil was at the right temperature. He could lift the frying basket, instantly assess, how much more time was needed, give the basket a quick shake, and re-immerse the food for the precise number of seconds. "Listen to the grease, Artie," was the mantra. "Listen to the grease." The result, quickly salted and served, was perfection-golden nuggets of bounty from the sea, naked, briny morsels from the North Atlantic, coated with pulverized grain from the heartland, plunged into rendered animal fat, and orchestrated by a maestro.

The seafood wholesale business went away, but the remaining restaurant was the better for it. His entire week's profit came in the few hours of demand provided by the Catholic church. "God Bless the Pope," Bull would say as he counted the receipts and the end of his Friday frying frenzy.

Bull knew all the nuances of fried fish--the right recipe for the batter, the precise temperature, everything. But what he really knew was fat. All fish fryers know that food tastes best when cooked in clean oil. Over time the fryers become cesspools of all that has been cooked before. When Bull looked into the cost factors of his business, he was surprised to find that fat, even more than fish, was the highest cost commodity in his business.

He could have done what most small restaurants do and just use the fat longer and longer, until a single piece of fish reveals the entire history of the summer. Or he could have kept the fat fresh, and raised his prices. Instead, he developed a simple pump and filter that cleaned the fat and extended its usable life. Not only did it reduce his operating costs, but it improved the quality and consistency of his fried foods. He called the device the Gordon Filtron®.

The take-out fish shop thrived, but Gordon's Sea Food was about to morph again. The owner of an ice cream stand in nearby Wollaston came to Bull to learn the secrets of his grease. He had just opened a restaurant and wanted to served golden fried clams, just like those that came from Bull's fryers. People were travelling more, he told Bull. They wanted familiar food in unfamiliar faces. His plan was to open restaurants with instantly recognizable orange roofs all over the country. And his name was Howard Johnson. Bull nodded, and agreed to outfit his fryers with Gordon Filtrons®

A few years later another local entrepreneur approached Bull. His business, a small coffee and donut shop, was only a few miles away. If Bull's fat filter could improve the flavor of Howard's fried clams, wouldn't it work with donuts, too? In not too many years Dunkin' Donuts were sprouting like weeds up and down the Eastern seaboard. The restaurant was closed down because it made more sense to manufacture Gordon Filtrons® than fish & chips. Bull's small place in fast food history was assured.

Bull Gordon's Seafood Chowder

To make a fish stock, take all of the clam shells, lobster shells, mussel or oyster shells, even fish bones if you have them and put them into an industrial-sized, stainless soup pot. Add left over bits of seafood-fish, clams, lobster. No fried food and no oily-fleshed fish (mackerel or bluefish). Add whatever you've got. It's not going to kill you.

Cut up two onions and several stocks of celery. Add several Bay leaves. Cover with water and bring to a boil. Boil for at least one half hour. Strain off stock.

Cube ¼ pound of salt pork and render in your soup pot. Peel and cut Maine potatoes into 1 inch slices. Cut onion to approximately the same size. Add both to pot. Stir until well coated. Add water to pot and bring to gentle boil. Cook until potatoes have lost their crunch.

Drain water and replace with fish stock. Bring to poaching temperature. Don't boil.

This is a dish that can accommodate just about any catch of the day, with the exception of oily fish. Flounder, hake, pollack, cod, haddock, skate are all fine Likewise just about any shellfish (shucked) will work, too. Cod's cheeks and tongues are particularly good.

Add it all, then let it simmer until seafood is cooked. Add 1 cup cream for every gallon of chowdah. Season with salt, pepper, dry sherry, and fresh green seasonings from the garden. Garnish with chopped parsley.

In some ways things didn't change. The families still came to Indian Mound each summer where Artie, his brother and sister, and countless cousins (including Cuzzin) spent seamless days chasing minnows and listening to Red Sox games and having seaweed fights and catching horseshoe crabs and playing mumblety-peg. Each day was capped by a lingering night of chasing fireflies, counting shooting stars, and re-telling family secrets. On Sundays the brothers Gordon would assemble their clan for potluck dinners. Sometimes it was franks and beans, brown bread, tomato aspic and Jello molds. More often, the bounty of the sea-steamers, mussels, battered flounder fillets, or Gordon's Seafood Chowder.

But times change, and so do people. Everyone was excited when Bull arrived at a Sunday dinner in his first Cadillac, but then he wasn't coming to the dinners as regularly. Business, don't you know. Then, there were family whispers and meetings from which the kids were excluded. Then, there was news that Bull had a fancy house in Florida, followed by the news that he was divorcing Aunt Jenn and marrying a new woman down there.

And so it came to pass that Cuzzin was sent to fancy, schmancy Milton Academy to be groomed as the heir to the Gordon family fortune. Artie was sent primarily to look after his little cousin. It may have been only the next town over, but it was light years from Indian Mound.

Artie fared well in prep school, going from Milton to Harvard (Harvard, for chrissakes!), then onto film school at UCLA, and his critically-acclaimed first film The King of California. Ten films later he was one of the most bankable directors in Hollywood , until *My Mother, My Lover*…. that is. In one swell foop his world came crashing down.

Cuzzin fared less well at Milton.. He was the youngest and rowdiest of the Gordonians. Maybe he had to be to get attention. It took him less than two years to get kicked out of Milton. By this time Artie was focused on his own life and was content to monitor reports from his Mother. Cuzzin was caught drinking. Cuzzin was kicked out of school. Cuzzin was in a barroom brawl. Cuzzin was married, then divorced. Cuzzin was in a motorcycle gang. Cuzzin caused a scene at his father's funeral. Cuzzin was taking the old seafood store and turning it into a bait & tackle shop.

On a dazzling April morning, two middle-aged men, one whose life has come full-circle and another who hasn't made it more than a stone's throw from Indian Mound share a beer.

Cuzzin's voice tells its own story. It's too loud, and the words come out in thick bunches. Every tire squeal, every cigarette, every shot of tequila can be heard. The voice is equal part seagull shriek and throaty moan of a Harley. It hangs in the air like cigarette smoke, even after he leaves the room.

Cuzzin reaches into the cooler and pulls out a fresh sixteen ounce Old Milwaukee Light for himself. "I try to keep one of these going all day. That way I always have a little buzz on, but nothin' so that I'm falling down drunk. You remember Tubby Tropiano?"

He silences the rock music that is filling the shop.

"He's now a cop. You believe that? One of Quincy's finest, and he'd like nothing better than to nail me for drunk driving, selling liquor without a license, whatever. Not that he and I aren't buddies, 'cause we are. He still lives on Indian Mound, the Donovan Place. But he'd nail me just to bust my chops and just because he's a dickhead cop. And so I make sure I stay nice and clean to bust his chops."

"Tubby Tropiano, a cop" muses Artie.

The two men observe each other, across the counter, through the beers, across the years.

"I thought of you about a month ago," said Cuzzin. "That broad on Channel 5, what's her name? Cynthia Twiddlecunt? Whatever. She reviewed your movie."

"That must have been interesting."

"Oh, did I say she 'reviewed' your movie. She 'assassinated' your movie, and you along with it." Cuzzin laughed. His laugh sounded like someone revving a motorcycle. Artie could recognize this laugh from when Cuzzin was a little nubber. With the benefit of hindsight, he could have predicted his cousin's future just from hearing the child laugh.

"I tried to see it, but even at the theaters that advertised it, they had all these wimps and bitches picketing it. It was in the news"

"And that's why I'm here," said Artie. "I want to lay low for a while and spend the summer at Indian Mound. I want to open up the cottage, and I'll probably need some help from you."

My Mother, My Lover...

Peopled stayed away from the movie in droves. They had to. Despite pre-release awards at the Cannes Film Festival and Sundance, a feeding frenzy was taking place even before the initial release date. It wasn't the film critics leading the charge, but rather the social activists looking to revitalize a flagging feminist movement. Seeing the changing tide, critics, talk show hosts, and other opinion makers climbed all over each other to mount the high horse of moral rectitude. The studio reacted by changing the trailers in the ad campaign to downplay what the movie was about, a naked examination of the changing roles of the sexes in contemporary culture, and to make it appear to be a screwball romantic comedy. This, in turn, so incensed the stars that when they went on their promotional junkets they spent more time ranting about the inanity of studio politics than talking about the film.

My Mother, My Lover... became a lightning rod for moral sanctity. Religious groups hopped on the bandwagon to show that they, too, were opposed to rampant moral turpitude. Ethnic groups came forward to protest that they were not equally included in this portrayal of rampant moral turpitude. Theaters and chains reacted to the tsunami of negative publicity by pulling the show with great fanfare. Some outlets even let the screen go dark. Instead of substituting another film, they donated the vacant theaters to high-minded non-profits for sensitivity workshops. The national news showed a battered women's organization in Albany that staged a fundraiser where people paid $25 for the privilege of sitting for two hours in a dark, silent theater not watching *My Mother, My Lover, My Ex-wife, My Lawyer, and Now My Sales Manager.* Afterwards, as the cameras rolled, there were the usual spates of pithy statements that CNN reduced to the soundbite of "Arthur Gordon just doesn't get it."

All of this occupied the national stage for just over two weeks in March, traditionally one of the dullest news periods of the year. As one anchorperson who interviewed Artie said, "It's too early for baseball; the snowstorms are old news; the tornadoes haven't started up; the mass murderers must go on Spring Break or something. We need people like you to fill up the news at this time of year."

"You can't stay there now."

"I don't intend to. I just want to check it out to. Then I fly to London and come back next week to move in."

Cuzzin's face darkens.

"What?" says Artie.

"There's no one been living at the cottage since your Mom died. What's it been, three years? No one's kept the place up at all. Listen, I've got some friends you can hire-"

"Nope. I've been hiring people to do my work for years so that I could be 'Arthur Gordon, Director.' Now, I want to manage my own shit. I'll stop back after I've scoped it out."

Return to the Mound

Arthur Gordon drives over the causeway that connects "Indian Mound" to the rest of the world feeling as if it is his bruised and battered body washing up on shore. The ordeal is past, but he's not yet sure whether or not he will survive, or whether he wants to.

Indian Mound is a small spit of dry land rising from a tidal marsh in Quincy Bay, a shallow subset of Boston Harbor. This was once a tidal island, connected to the Squantum peninsula only at low tide. As he drives over the causeway, the salt air arouses Artie's earliest memories of walking to The Mound when it was accessible only by foot.

Can I really remember that? Or have I created the memory from retelling the story so many times. So much has changed. So much is the same. Every house but mine is now winterized. This doesn't even pretend to be a summer community. The skyline of Boston seems close enough to touch. I remember when the John Hancock was the tallest building. We looked at the light for our weather forecast. The second tallest was the old Custom House. With a telescope you could read the clock. It wasn't enough for a building to be a building. There had to be a higher purpose. Now, it's enough to be a magnificent building.

The time was. The time is. Snot-nosed Artie, eight years old, barefoot for the entire summer still exists. Indian Mound still exists as a place that doesn't need satellite dishes or SUVs clogging its three narrow streets. It doesn't need video games or designer water. It needs clams and summer breezes and greased watermelon fights. It needs campfires and marshmallows and night games from Kansas City.

Kansas City was the westernmost city in the American League back then. It was as if the country ended there. Sure, Los Angeles and San Francisco and Seattle existed, but they were too new for major league baseball.

"Oh God, I am old," mutters Artie as his rental car reaches the end of the causeway and officially enters The Mound.. "And I am living in the past, and I am thinking all the thoughts of an old fart."

I don't know if I can do this. I can stop right here, right now. Do a U-turn, go back to Logan, catch the first flight back to LA. Go first class, because I can. I am still Arthur Gordon, Hollywood poohbah. I can still take a good shot to the body and that's what this is, a good body shot. I just made an unpopular film, that's all.

Two boys were shooting baskets listlessly on a mobile, adjustable backboard. Both were dressed in oversized replica jerseys bearing the names of NBA stars. Their court was the street, forcing Artie to stop. Even with the backboard adjusted to its lowest level, the boys were unable to reach the rim without the assisted boost from a strategically-placed stump. They were in no hurry to move the stump so that the car could pass.

No, for chrissakes. You don't play basketball on Indian Mound. Basketball is for winter and city. You play baseball or some facsimile thereof. You make up games with a tennis ball and you use your hand for a bat. If you don't have a tennis ball you make a ball out of rolled up socks and rubber bands. You draw the bases in the sand with your toe, and then when they are obscure you argue about every single call so that everyone can claim victory. You don't need to dunk and you don't need to wear a $65 logo jersey with an ad for Reebok on it. You don't need this crap and that paraphernalia and if you are going to wear colors they *damn well better be the kelly green of the Celtics. At least they are the one team with character, and they are your goddamn hometown team.*

Artie flashed on himself not less than a month ago, attending a Lakers game, flashing the hi sign to Jack Nicholson and taking note of what good company he was keeping. Jack kidded him about being the "little, fat, bald guy" with "the Oriental Swede" as he referred to Meiko, Artie's girl friend. Artie took it in stride. Hey, when Nicholson treats you like a locker room buddy, you roll with the punches. He knew that people noticed him more because he had a blond, Chinese bimbo bombshell on his arm. Plus, he was trashtalking with Jack. Hey, that's what it's all about, right? Being famous enough to act like a normal person.

The first time he attended a Lakers game, he was offended by the sideshows and that trivialized the actual game. This wasn't Boston Garden, with its parquet and dusty rafters with the retired jerseys of champions. The Garden had dignity. It was a cathedral. In L.A. you spend the first quarter seeing who else is there. Then, you spend the second quarter figuring out what to eat. Then, at halftime, it's a mad rush to shake hands with everyone above you in the pecking order. In the third quarter, you leave to beat the traffic. If you're a real fan, you find out who wins on the radio.

As time passed and Artie's status rose, and his seating improved to four rows behind the bench, he came to enjoy the ritual. Now, instead of spending his time tracking down the other celebrities in attendance, he let them find him.

Now, he was smiling beatifically at two boys taking their sweet time about rolling their stump out of the way so that his rented Lincoln could pass. "This fuckin'sucks," he muttered through lips pursed in an utterly false display of patience. "Little twerps."

The Lincoln stops. Artie gets out to stare at the forlorn little cottage. Even the brightness of the day is diminished by the overgrowth. So, this is what three years of neglect will do. Artie walks to the front door, "climbs" is more like it, reaches up over the light and finds the key still in its familiar place. The windows are boarded. The paint, as on Cuzzin's Bait & Tackle, is peeling.

The lawn hasn't been mowed in three years. Three years of leaves have accumulated. The bushes are three years larger. Three years is a long time in the world of a small cottage.

"I'm in a bad dream," says Artie. Then he opens the front door. "The dream just got worse," he says as he surveys a dark, cobwebby room, with all the furniture covered in plastic. The place is in shambles. Animals have gotten into some of the overstuffed furniture and made nests. The critters reign. Artie blows the dust off a family photo and picks up a small sailboat, one that was his as a boy.

I can turn around right now. In one half-hour I can be checking in to the Ritz and calling room service to send up a Beefeater Gibson, straight-up. I can be on the telephone to Meiko. I can check my emails.

"Otty. Hiyo, Ot-tee! You in there?" Artie comes back out into the sunlight. He sees a police officer, wearing his blues. He is about Artie's age, but bigger all over. He peers through thirty years and sees Tubby Tropiano.

"Oh, sweet Jesus, do I have to call you 'Officer?'"

"You can call me 'Asshole.' I heard you was down here! I had to come see for myself. Hey, you're looking good. Old, but good." The two men shake hands, then embrace. Artie stands back to take in the whole spectacle.

"*Officer* Tropiano. How did this come to pass?"

"I got outta the service and didn't know what to do. I've been doing this for fifteen years, retire in five. Where you been? Off in Hollywood making movies"

"Making *lousy* movies."

"I like your movies, but I didn't get to see this last one. Seemed too much like a chick flic. What are you doing here?"

"I'm here for the summer."

"You're kidding! We hardly see you for thirty years and now you're here for the summer? You staying in the cottage."

"That's the idea." Officer Tropiano reacted with a wince.

"Needs a bit of work."

"Yes, it's primitive, but that's part of the appeal."

"You want to stay with me and the missus. You know we live right over on Sea Shell Road. Remember the Donovan Place?"

"I do. Let me give this a try, and if it's too bad, it's good to know you're there."

"You know who I married?"

"No, who?"

"Kathleen Sullivan."

"Kathleen Sullivan? She gave me my first hand job!"

And in an instant, Officer Tropiano became a twelve year old Tubby, swearing and mock punching at Artie Gordon just as they had many years ago.

Codfish Cakes
A Recipe from Lucille Gordon (Artie's Mom)

This is really a tough one. I'm sure this recipe evolved back in the days when a cheap source of protein was needed to nourish the slaves working the sugarcane plantations in the Caribbean. Codfish from the Grand Banks were dried and salted on the shores of Newfoundland. The desiccated flesh was then packed into wooden barrels and shipped south

Even as a kid we always kept a wooden box of salt cod from Canada in the cupboard, either for rainy days or that special Sunday morning breakfast. The codfish cakes were always served with baked beans.

Now, however, the cod fishery has collapsed, overfished by generations and nationalities. This was the resource that truly seemed limitless, but we proved once again that the greed and voraciousness of the human species cannot be denied. Salt cod is now a delicacy that cost more per pound than fresh lobster. Even worse, the little wooden boxes that remind you of days gone past are products of China.

Codfish cakes make no sense at all anymore. But they do remind me.

Soak 1 pound dried cod overnight. Drain.

Peel and boil six medium potatos

Finely dice one medium sized cooking onion

Mash potatoes in mixing bowl. Add other ingredients.

Salt and pepper to taste

Add two heaping tablespoons of grated horseradish.

Cut 4 ounces of salt pork into small, ¼ inch cubes.

Render in a cast iron frying pan until pork bits have browned.

On his way out of town, Artie stops at Cuzzin's Bait & Tackle.

"Change your mind on hiring some help?"

"No," says Artie. "I'm pretty determined to do this myself, but I do have a deal for you."

"When I get back in a week, how about we swap vehicles for a while. I've got a feeling I'll be making a few trips to the dump."

"I always pictured myself in a Lincoln."

Arthur Gordon's Beefeater Gibson

Store a bottle of Beefeater Gin in the freezer. Approximately ten minutes before you serve drinks, invert stemmed martini glasses in the freezer to chill. Put cracked (not crushed, not cubed) ice made with distilled water into a stainless steel beaker. Add 3 ounces of gin for each Gibson. Shake like hell. Place beaker on counter. Take out glasses and add 4 small cocktail onions to each glass. Strain gin into frosty glasses. Take out dry white Vermouth bottle (any brand) and hold near to glasses. Make a wise-ass comment like "Eat your heart out, sucker" or "Ha-ha-ha-ha-ha." Replace Vermouth bottle in liquor cabinet. Under no circumstances even open it. Drink no more than one of these, or you are asking for trouble.

Chapter 2 - His Familiar

Sandy Beach's Fishing Forecast for May:
Stripers Return to Boston Harbor

This is what we've been waiting for. This is what we live for. The harsh winter and early spring are over, the "stripahs," in the local inflection, are returning to the harbor with a vengeance. Herring are finding their ways into all the area rivers-the Charles, the Neponset, Black's Creek-and the bass are right behind them. Good fishing has been reported in Winthrop, Hingham Bay, the Charles River Locks, and the Amelia Earhart Dam. This coming week will see stripers appearing in good numbers and sizes in most places with structure. No big fish yet, but there's a lot of fun to be had on light tackle. Just about any baitfish imitation will do.

Now's a good time to take a day off from work to go chase them.

-Sandy Beach, from The Boston Globe

A Good Sub

A quick trip to London. *My Mother, My Lover.....* is doing modestly well. Brits can't understand the controversy. An ordinary man is engaged, overwhelmed, and eventually victimized by the women in his life. What's the big deal? Artie is interviewed in *Time Out Magazine*. The interviewer asks him about camera angles and lighting choices. Artie fields them deftly, and feels that maybe he has turned the corner. When his plane lands, however, it is right in the middle of a shitstorm of tabloid reporters. Who was the real-life model for the lawyer? What did he have to say about Cameron Diaz saying she had been "tricked" into doing the movie? Had he heard about the viewer response to the *60 Minutes* interview?

Artie plunges toward the cottage, stopping only to swap vehicles with Cuzzin. OK, he gulps beer. He has worked out his strategy on the plane ride. First, make a place to sleep. Then, get the services-electricity, gas, and water-connected. Regroup. Buy tools and supplies. Restore the cottage to its simple summer glory as it exists in his memory. He thinks he can have everything done by Memorial Day.

The same two kids are playing basketball. They regard him with trepidation. A stranger has come to town. His presence won't be unnoticed in a small community like Indian Mound.

A pale green has infused the vegetation. The forsythia is brilliant, but needs to be trimmed. Spring has sprung.

"Trim forsythia. I'll make that as #72 on the to-do list," Artie tells himself.

Inside the cottage, his first goal is light. He unshutters the windows, then begins to drag rugs and furniture out onto the lawn. The air is dank and musty. The insects regard him with the same expressions as the kids on the street.

"Get used to it," says Artie aloud. "There's a new kid in town, and you're going to have to make room, because he ain't going away."

After two hours, the shamble of the cottage has grown to become the shamble of the front yard. Each step backward is accompanied by two more steps backward. He unrolls a braided rug, and frees a family of mice who have nested with the material that used to be the rug's center. Throw it in the truck. It looks like a trip to the landfill has moved up on the priority list.

Things break or don't work. Little things like door latches and windows. Stopping to fix each one takes time. The tools he has to work with are rusted and ravaged by years of exposure to salt water and general neglect. Moreover, for most of his adult life Artie has lived in a world where other people have taken care of his basic survival needs. He is hopelessly deficient in basic life skills. He can manage a cast of thousands and bring a hundred million-dollar film in on time and on budget, but he doesn't really understand how a window works.

His eyes betray him. The last time he spent time on Indian Mound he hadn't needed glasses. Now they are essential every time he needs to band a nail or turn a screw. The glasses are on and off. He loops them into his shirt, sticks them in his pocket, places them a convenient flat surface. He spends half his time looking for his glasses. And it's only a matter of time until he breaks them. Two steps back.

By lunchtime Artie has accumulated enough refuse in Cuzzin's truck to warrant a trip to the dump. His spirits brighten. It's a beautiful day, and he will accomplish something by getting rid of a truckload of moldy crap. Plus, it's liberating to be driving a battered old truck. He stops at a sub sandwich shop and orders himself a large meatball with the works.

"Do you have a rest room?"

"Sorry, no."

Oh, shit. I'm going to have to eat my sandwich with hands that have spent the morning in spiderwebs and mouse turds? Artie put on an expression of vulnerability and helplessness.

"Uh, well, you can come back here and use the utility sink."

"Heh-heh-heh-heh," smiles Artie to himself. Who's the actor and who's the director here?

Artie drives to a small turnoff just off Ocean Avenue where he can look out at the Bay and the islands of Boston Harbor. He used to know all their names. Let's see, that one's Peddocks, and that's Rainsford or maybe Georges Island. There's a Civil War fort there. And the little one is Hangman's, and behind it is Long Island. He is proud that so many names come back to him.

Only a month ago he was a regular at Spago's. Wolfgang Puck would come out to greet him whenever he went into his restaurant. At his favorite sushi joint they would bring him a plate of his custom creations (none of them even on the regular menu!) automatically. All he had to do was sit at his regular table. Enough people were turned onto his plate that you could now order "the Arthur Gordon Special."

Damn, this is a good sub, thought Artie. He didn't even mind that he was wearing the sandwich on his pants.

At the landfill he was stopped by a very fat man perched precariously on a plastic folding chair.

"Where's your sticker?"

"I need a sticker? Looks like I don't have one."

"Resident of Quincy?"

"Yes, I am. I've got a summer cottage down-"

"Identification?"

"I've got identification, but it won't show me as a resident of Quincy."

"How about a tax bill?"

34

"Not with me."

"A piece of mail addressed to you at your Quincy address?"

"No."

"Any way to prove you're a resident of Quincy?"

"Just my word."

"Well, then, you're shit out of luck."

Artie blew out a sigh of frustration and reached for his wallet, extracting a twenty and waving out the driver's side window. "Can't I just pay a fee?"

This provoked the man to laboriously extract his mass from the chair and to lumble (a combination of lumber and waddle) to the truck.

"What do I look like to you?" he asked Artie. "A fat slob," immediately came to mind, but Artie settled for the more diplomatic:

"A guy doing his job."

"Very good," said the man. "Excellent. And do you know what my job is? My job is to enforce the rules. The rules are very simple. To use the landfill you need to be a resident of Quincy and you need to purchase a sticker for a measly ten dollars to give you unlimited use of the dump and recycling center. If you don't have a sticker, but you can prove you are a resident of Quincy, you can use the facilities for a fee of $5 per use. You have neither a sticker nor proof of residency, therefore, you can't use the landfill."

"Oh, come on," protested Artie, "Just take the twenty and let me dump this stuff."

"Do I look like a corrupt civil servant to you?"

Artie jammed the truck into reverse and tried to show his disgust by spinning up a cloud of dust with his exit. He muttered all the way to Cuzzin's Bait & Tackle, where he amused his cousin immensely with his description of the encounter.

When he finally stopped laughing, Cuzzin grabbed a fresh beer, turned the sign on the front window to "Closed."

"Are we going back there?" You bet, said Cuzzin. Gonna talk some sense with this guy.

Cuzzin took the wheel and they retraced Artie's route to the landfill. The truck stopped next to the fat man perched on his plastic throne. "Hey, you fat wuss" growled Cuzzin. "I got a guy here who wants to rip off your head and take a shit in your neck."

The man approached the truck with what Artie saw as uncontrolled menace. Cuzzin held his ground. As he reached the vehicle he said, "Hey, Fuck Face." The men tapped fists.

"Howyadoin', Knobby? This here's my cousin Artie. He grew up with me on Indian Mound."

"Howyadoin', Artie?" said Knobby, the menace gone.

"Howyadoin'?" reflected Artie.

Cuzzin and Knobby exchanged pleasantries about how ugly the other was, with various side comments about the other's sexual inadequacy. Artie just soaked it all in. Finally, Cuzzin said, "So what do we have to do to get rid of this shit?"

"Just dump it over there," said Knobby.

"Thanks, man."

"No problem."

"I'll probably be bringing up more stuff," said Artie. "Where do I get a sticker?"

"Ahh, don't bother. So long as you're haulin' shit in Cuzzin's truck I'll wave you right through."

They dumped their load. On the way out, Knobby waved. "Nice meetin' ya, Artie."

"You've made a friend," said Cuzzin.

Artie and Cuzzin arranged to meet for dinner that night at Anna's, which used to be called Jack Colton's when they were growing up.

The Question of Beer for Breakfast

Back at the cottage Artie looks at the unsightly mess of the front lawn. He is way behind where he expected to be. Before plunging back in, he monitors the messages on his cell phone:

> ➤ His agent wants to know if he is interested in speaking to the National Press Club on the issue of fairness in the media.

> ➤ A representative for *Imus in the Morning*. Calls to see if he'd like to appear on the show.

> ➤ His son Liam calls to see if he is ready for him to come down and help at the cottage. Liam is just finishing up his next-to-last semester at the Berklee School of Music, and has just taken a job working second shift at a Dunkin Donuts baking plant.

> ➤ Meiko calls to remind him that he is the world's best lover, with the world's biggest penis. She tells him his house in Hollywood is fine and asks when can she come visit him in Boston.

> ➤ Mike Wallace's executive assistant calls to say that Mike sends his thanks and hopes he liked the finished 60 Minutes piece. The ratings were excellent.

> ➤ Jim Giberti, his longtime associate producer, expresses rage and sympathy over *60 Minutes*, and mentions that he has signed on to help Michael Bay produce the new *Men in Black IV*.

The only call he answers is Liam's. Liam, wearing a hairnet and white smock with a Dunkin' Donuts logo, is on a break from his new job of frying glazed donuts. He is slight and dark, with the heavily tattooed arms of a fledgling rock star. He is smoking a cigarette. Artie sits in a wicker chair that he has dragged out onto the lawn. The cottage is in close proximity to other houses. Right next door, separated by a low picket fence, a woman in a leotard is going through the slow motions of Tai Chi exercises to the sounds of soft classical music. Artie watches her as he speaks:

"Liam. Wuddup? It's your Papa. Finished with exams? How'd they go? Yeah, I'm here right now, at the cottage, sitting in the front yard that hasn't been mowed for three years, watching this weird babe next door do one of those slow motion kung fu things. This place definitely could use your help. In fact, it can use all the help it can get, but not yet. Right now it's an embarrassment, and I'd rather you didn't see it this way. Give me today and tomorrow to get the first layer of filth off, then come down on Friday. By then I should have electricity, water-you know, the basic conveniences of 19th century life. Until then, I might as well be camping out. Actually, camping out would be a big step up from what I'm doing right now. Have they given you your work schedule? Good. Call me again tomorrow. Hey, guess what, I'm having dinner with your Uncle Cuzzin tonight. Do you even remember him? What a piece of work. See ya soon."

Here was Liam's side of the conversation:

"Hello. Hey! Ooooo, Poppa's a rapper!. Yeah, O.K. Uh-huh. O.K. I have Fridays and Tuesdays off. Cool! Sure I do. I will. Seeya."

Artie closed his phone and lingered on the woman in her languid world of slow motion. She's has made a ton of improvements to the house next door. The grounds are immaculate. Even though it is early spring, the gardens show promise. Various Buddahs and garden statuary maintain a serene vigil over the plants. The contrast to his mounting pile of rubble is clear and dramatic. He gets back to work.

When the houses of Indian Mound were built, it made sense for them to be small and close together. Everyone who lived there was escaping the fetid heat of summer in the city.

Compared to the mattress out onto the fire escape, a cottage by the water was heaven. Although less than ten miles from South Boston, Dorchester, Jamaica Plain, or West Roxbury, Indian Mound was graced by seaside breezes that was a tonic for sleeping. Think of it--your own little, separate cottage, with trees for shade and even a patch of grass. C'mon, don't get no better.

Originally part of the estate owned by the John Quincy Adams family, Indian Mound was sold to a real estate speculator named Christian Dunham who promptly divided the acreage into small lots separated by streets with romantic, beachy names-Sea Shell Road, Sand Dollar Lane, Cormorant Alley. The small lots of Indian Mound, advertised as "healthful, seaside sites, perfect for villas or bungalows" were snapped up by the middle class gentry of greater Boston who could now afford a second home. It was such a good situation that you shared it with the people closest to you, brothers and sisters. Four Gordon brothers and three cousins purchased lots on Indian Mound, making it an instant family enclave. After two generations of displacement and emigration, they had been gradually separated by jobs and the demands of upward mobility. This was a perfect way to connect for a few precious weeks in the New England summer.

The cottages were built within several summers. Indian Mound became a frenzy of lumber and banging nails. As soon as there was a roof, you moved in. If you didn't know everyone already, you would soon, because the lots were so small that you could sit in your front lawn and see six or eight neighbors. But who cared about privacy? You had an ocean on one side and a salt marsh on three others. Collectively, the residents of Indian Mound had all the privacy needed to live a carefree summer life. Windows were opened, doors unlocked, and clothes shed. You could walk into anyone's house without knocking. You could hear anyone's conversation. You shared their lives, for better or for worse.

Artie remembered the big fight that Tubby Tropiano's parents had over whether or not it was all right for Tubby's Dad to drink a beer in the morning. Mrs. Tropiano thought this was the height of dereliction and the first step towards perdition. Mr. Tropiano, however, defended himself by saying it was only a beer, for chrissakes, and after all, he was on vacation that week and should be able to do whatever the hell he pleased. Everyone on the Mound took sides, and while the lines were generally drawn on gender lines, there was enough crossover to insure this would be a topic of debate for at least two summers.

The construction of the causeway in 1955 marked the end of The Mound as a summer community. Cars appeared on the dusty streets. Then, the dusty streets were paved. Then, people started winterizing their cottages. The casualty was summer.

The houses were expanded and winterized throughout the Fifties, but since they were built on such small footprints, the expansions went up and out, often at odd and awkward angles. Instead of screened in porches designed to let in the cooling summer breezes, fortresses were constructed to keep out the harsh elements of the North Atlantic winter. Decisions were made based on where to put the TV rather than where you could see the sunset. Overstuffed leather couches now dominated rooms designed for airy wicker. The porches were enclosed and climate-controlled with air conditioners. Expansion could go in only one direction, up. The graceful lines of the cottages have been lost. Now, Indian Mound is a summer community on steroids.

Added to the sense of congestion are the roads, choked with SUVS, two per bloated cottage. Artie wonders if a Lincoln Navigator is really essential to life on Indian Mound.

Shea Provost

The cleaner (relatively speaking) the cottage became, the messier the lawn. Artie brought a braided rug out onto the lawn, hung it over a line, and started whacking it with a good, old fashioned rug beater that he had found. Whap, whap, whap! Each sound brought a satisfying puff of dust.

"Do you really think you can beat something into cleanliness?"

Artie turned around to see the Tai Chi lady leaning on the fence. He guessed her to be about his age, but well preserved and in better shape. Her expression was not welcoming.

"This is how we've always cleaned the rugs. Beat the dust out and let the sun dry them out." Artie gave a few more whacks. "Look at that," he said, gesturing proudly to his last dust cloud.

"You're dealing in levels of filth that I can't relate to. I guess I don't see the point." She didn't wait for a response.

Shea Provost's perspective: I've busted my fucking butt to make something of myself. I excelled in high school and college. I kept my nose clean. I worked a free internship. I endured unwanted sexual passes from my bosses and undeserved catty comments from tight-assed secretaries for the opportunity to work fourteen hours a day for despicable clients whose only virtue was that they could pay our bills. I have been a highly polished professional prostitute and I have done it damn well so that I could get the financial independence to get me own little house in a safe, quiet neighborhood where I could have a little peace and privacy. Now, some buffoon who owns the shack next door, which should just disintegrate into the marsh, comes by to make his front lawn look like a yard sale. To make matters worse, he has to advertise his presence with his repeated thwock-thwocking of a rug that should be put out into the trash. I wonder if I should call the authorities.

By nightfall Artie has applied a veneer of civility to the cottage, a very thin veneer. Cuzzin comes by, holding the pre-requisite beer plus one for Artie, and takes the nickel tour.

Cuzzin's thoughts: This place is a museum of memories. I can tell you a story about each piece of furniture and knickknack. But it is so run down! I can't see anyone living here. I couldn't even see me living here, and I'm the world's biggest slob. Artie should just tear it down before it falls down. What's going on in his head? God bless him. I'm hungry. Let's eat.

"Are you really going to stay here?"

"Yeah."

"You don't even have any water. What if you have to take a dump?"

"I'll figure something out. They're turning on the water in the morning. Can I call you if there are any leaks?"

"Yeah, sure. Hungry?"

Anna's of Squantum

They have dinner at Anna's of Squantum, the restaurant that was Jack Colton's when they were growing up. Coming here was a once a summer treat. Cuzzin works the bar area as if he is running for office.

"Cuzzin! Any stripers in the Bay, yet?"

"Is that truck still on the road?"

"You break your bike out of mothballs yet!"

"I haven't seen you since the night Tubby Tropiano busted us."

"You know what you should do? Start selling those sea kayaks."

Cuzzin's distinctive laugh, which sounds like a revved motorcycle, energizes the room. People buy him drinks. He buys a round. The Sox are playing Baltimore. There's a six-nothing lead for the home team. All is right with the world.

Eventually, they are seated. Artie orders the fried fisherman's platter. It arrives as a golden mound, with fish, shrimp, scallops, and clams piled high on a bed of French fries. Cuzzin orders littlenecks on the half shell, followed by the fried clam plate.

"I feel like I'm eating my inventory," he says, vroom, vroom, vrooming at his own joke.

Not much of Jack Colton's can be seen in Anna's, although the entrance to the kitchen is still in the same place. The smoke-stained paneling has been replaced with new paneling, which is now being smoke stained. The people seem roughly the same, however. Come to think of it, the food is just about the same.

"I'm not complaining, but you just can't get fried fish as good as Bull's," says Artie. "But, of course, in Hollywood eating fried food is a sin that ranks up with pedaphilia or gang rape. What kind of wine is appropriate with fried shit?"

"All you'll get here is red, pink, or white. I'd recommend something with bubbles."

"Is there anyplace that serves fried seafood as good as Bull's"

"Nah!" says Cuzzin emphatically, "Not even close. These clams spent about ten seconds too long in the fat. Ten seconds ain't much, but in the world of world class frying, ten seconds is a lot. I also find the batter too heavy. And while we're being critical, the cole slaw needs vinegar."

"They didn't 'listen to the grease.'"

"Exactly. They didn't 'listen to the grease.'"

Artie chimed in "I don't like the way they served the seafood on top of the fries. It makes for an impressive looking plate, but by the time you reach the fries, they've blotted up the grease from the fish."

"That's why paper containers are perfect for fried food. They insulate, but absorb."

"Now that my career as a Hollywood mogul is down the tubes, maybe I can get back into being a fryer of fish."

That's good for a vroom or two.

The two men compare their worlds.

"You gotta tell me one thing," says Cuzzin with bits of clam batter clinging to his muzzle. "You ever fuck anybody famous?"

Artie looked left and right, to make sure they were alone in the din. He took a sip of his drink. "Yup, I fucked Harrison Ford." That was good enough to fill the room with Cuzzin's laugh. Suddenly everyone had to know the punchline, and Cuzzin repeated it, as he would to bait shop customers for the next month.

"How about starlets. Is it true they'll do anything to get a break?"

"You'll get to meet a starlet in a couple of weeks. My girl-friend Mieko's coming as soon as I get the cottage fixed up. You can ask her?"

"What movies has she been in?" asked Artie.

"The only one so far is *My Mother, My Lover*, and that was just a walk-on bit that I threw in to shut her up. But to answer your question, everyone in Los Angeles is desperate to see their name in lights and face on the big screen-it's true for guys and girls. And they will do anything, anything, for someone who is in position to move them up a step on the latter. It's an American cliché and it's totally pathetic and completely true."

Cuzzin took it all in with knowing nods of comprehension, then said in a tone that reflected Artie, "It's the same in the bait business."

Cuzzin's turn for storytelling arrived, and he had a long tale to tell. It was a tale where each new chapter began in response to the fuck-up that ended the last. His parents kicked him out of the house because of the many miscapades of his late teen-age years. Then, they moved off to Florida after his father scored with Howard Johnson and Dunkin' Donuts, leaving Cuzzin the former fish shop, by that time a lawyer's office where all the lawyers bitched about the smell. He considered restarting the seafood and restaurant business, but there was no remaining equipment and the Pope had relaxed the ban on eating meat on Friday. The only thing people wanted to eat was hamburgers.

Besides life was complicated. He married the wrong girl for the wrong reasons with the predictable results. He kicked out the lawyers and opened the bait business where he didn't have to worry about things like the board of health.

"I never did anything with my life, Artie. You don't know this, but I once rode my bike out to California to see if you could get me a job in the movies. When I got there, I was too chicken to call you up. I sat in a Motel 6 for two days paralyzed with fear, then got back on my bike and rode back to Indian Mound. Here I am."

Here you are, ensconced in a cozy little place where everyone knows and loves you. I can go to The Brown Derby for lunch and be approached by ten strangers who will introduce themselves and try to hustle me for their personal scams. I get mobbed at halftime at the Laker's games. I have to hire people to screen my calls. Even now, my agent is dealing with all the media who want to fry my ass. But I'm actually the loser in the family, not you. The winners stay home because they can. The losers are the pioneers. And the pioneers, no matter what they say, are lonely. Who do you think stayed home in the family castle in Scotland? The winners. Who got on a leaky ship to cross the North Atlantic? The losers who have nothing to lose. That's why they're called "losers."

The men let the silence talk for several moments, letting their souls reacquaint after years of separation. Finally, the cosmos align.

"What do you know about the old babe who lives next to me?"

"You interested?" Cuzzin' raises a lecherous eyebrow.

"Are you kidding? Wait until you meet Meiko. I've been spoiled by the willing starlets. I wouldn't know what to do with an old broad. Jesus, she must be my age."

"Personally, I find her to be a piece of ass. The best thing about getting old is that the young babes look just as good, but the old ones get much better looking. Her name is Shea something, and she's some kind of executive professional type who works in an office in downtown Boston, and she's really into yoga and meditation and all that crunchy, groovy stuff. When she looks at me, it's like she's looking at something she found crawling underneath her garbage can." Cuzzin paused for a moment of self-examination, "Jeez, I can't understand that!"

"She was pretty condescending to me today. I think she's very annoyed to see someone at the cottage. Oh well, we'll win her over. Tomorrow's a big day. The water gets turned on. Think of it, running water, right inside the house."

"What will they think of next?" said Cuzzin.

Artie swaddles himself in a sleeping bag on the wicker couch in the main room. In the darkness, however, it becomes apparent that the house belongs to the critters. He feels beady eyes upon him. He hears skittering and scratching. He thinks he sees long, tapered tails disappearing around corners. Finally, after several near panic attacks, he lights a candle that he puts next to him in the middle of a metal platter. Ensconced by some of the trappings of civilization, he drifts off to troubled sleep, surrounded by his familiar.

I'm lying in a wooden shack with rodents skittering over my sleeping bag. Two months ago I was at the Cannes Film Festival with Meiko. People cared what I thought about life and art, politics, religion. They cared because I was Arthur Gordon. I was Arthur Gordon.

Bull Gordon's Fried Fish Perfection

The perfect piece of fish to fry is the thicker end of the fillet from a 3-4 pound haddock. Cod is excellent, too, as is flounder, but haddock is the ultimate.

The best oil to use is lard, which will give your fish a deep gold appearance and will impart a slight nutty flavor to the crust. Heat the fat to 370 degrees. Use only clean fat that is kept squeaky clean due to the continuous filtration of Gordon's Fat Filtrator. Monitor the temperature with a thermometer, or test by dropping in a one-inch cube of bread. It should brown in one minute.

Dip fillet in a bowl of cold, evaporated milk, then toss into bowl of fry mix.

To make Gordon's Fry Mix sift together 1 cup corn flour, 1 cup all purpose flour, ½ cup powdered whey, 1 teaspoon salt and ½ teaspoon baking powder.

Shake to remove all excess fry mix and place fillets in wire basket. Do not overcrowd, as fat needs to move freely between pieces. The fat will sputter and hiss when fish is first added. When the sound becomes softer and less bubbly, lift out for visual inspection. There is a short period of time when the batter goes from gold to deep gold. Remove from heat. Shake to drain, salt lightly, and serve on a paper plate or boat. Accompany with lemon wedge, Gordon's cole slaw, and Gordon's tartar sauce.

Chapter 3 - Wicked Bad

Light came late the next morning. After hours of rodent-induced anxiety, Artie falls into a deep slumber. It is nearly nine o'clock when he awakes, then another half-hour until he has the courage to leave the warmth of the sleeping bag. He drives to the nearest Dunkin' Donuts and orders the #1 with a large coffee with two glazed donuts. He wonders if Liam made these donuts. When prompted by the clerk, Artie confirms that he wants his coffee "regular" (pronounced "regg-a-lah") only to find that "regular" means equal parts coffee, cream, and sugar. By that time he returns to the Mound and finishes his breakfast, the fried seafood platter that he enjoyed so much at Anna's has worked its way through his stomach and is currently residing impatiently in his lower intestine.

Artie has to take a dump. Wicked bad.

He reviews the options. He could walk over to Tropiano's, introduce himself to the Mrs., and then say, "I know we haven't seen each other in thirty-five years, but I gotta take a dump, wicked bad."

He could drive up to Cuzzin's, but he guesses that the chance of him being there this early is no better than 50/50. He could drive up to one of the fast food joints on the Southern Artery, but his gut is telling him that might be risky.

He could go out to the back yard and squat, but with the houses on the Mound packed so tightly together, there is no place that affords complete privacy, and his neighborhood status would hardly be enhanced if anyone saw him. The way his luck was running lately, someone would have a camera handy and he'd find a shot of himself pooping on the cover of the National Enquirer.

If only the water department would show up.

Water! Artie has his answer. A toilet works by gravity. That much he knows. In order to get a single flush, all he needs to do is to fill the toilet tank with a few gallons of water. He can get a bucket of water from a neighbor's garden hose and pour it in the toilet tank!

Chortling at his own ingenuity, Artie finds a large pot used for boiling lobsters and quickly locates a garden hose on the house of the woman next door. He briefly considers knocking, but knowing that he is unkempt and unshaven, and that she works in Boston and would by now be safely ensconced in her downtown skyscraper, he opts for helping himself. Encouraged by his creativity, and motivated by the continued downward passage of his fried seafood dinner, Artie sleuths across to her porch and turns on the hose. He is a man with a plan. The peristaltic waves are coming more frequently now. "Hurry up, please, it's time," he says to the hose. Next time at Anna's, he vows, he'd have his seafood platter broiled.

He jumps at the sound of her voice.

"What do you think you're doing?

She is on her deck. He is on the ground about three feet below. He looks up into a face that registers midway between disgust and alarm, as if she had just found something slimy and alive underneath her garbage can. This, Artie decides, calls for boyish innocence:

"Oh, hi! I'm Artie. That's my cottage. I didn't think you were home, so I didn't bother to knock. My water isn't turned on yet, so I thought it would be ok for me to borrow some from you." *"Borrow?" Did I really say "borrow?" As if I'm going to come back tonight with a lobster pot of water, and say "Here's your water I'm returning."*

"I'm not working these days, and it's not ok, ever, to come onto my property and to touch anything without my permission."

"Guilty as charged. You're absolutely right!" Artie tries to give his grin an infectious quality. He can hear himself describing the look to one of his actors. He was great at coaxing out the best from his actors. But his actors usually weren't holding heavy pots of water while trying to stem the urgency of peristalsis. "I'm sorry. I really am. But I really need this water. And I really need it now." His gut was cramping painfully.

"Let's set some clear boundaries right now, and we can start by you pouring out the water." The "boyish" part of his act must have worked, because she was treating him like a naughty boy.

"And I'm glad to have this discussion, but not at this exact moment."

"Conflicts are always best resolved when issues are addressed immediately."

"Not when one of the parties is in extreme gastric distress."

"Come again?"

"I've got to take a dump, wicked bad," says Artie, turning with his pot and walking purposefully towards the cottage. Behind him he hears the crackle of a bridge burning.

The Garden Bitch

Ah, relief. As he prepares to start his day, Artie catches a glimpse of himself in the mirror. Whoa! Scary! He had never seen himself look so disheveled. His head was bleary, gray, and random. "No wonder what's-her-name looked so alarmed." He spends part of the morning obsessing about her name, finally convincing himself that it is "Shawna." He'd charm her the next time he'd see her. No need for bad blood between neighbors. He'd show her the real Arthur Gordon.

The water department arrives on schedule. The city worker is curious to see that there is still a summer cottage still left in Quincy. Artie shows him around. Artie is already taking pride in the slight progress he has made, but the water department person is more amazed than impressed. He appears unable to grasp the concept of a summer cottage, finally reducing it to "kinda like a tent."

"That's it," says Artie, "A big wooden tent."

"I gotta run. Do you want to try the water before I go."

Artie goes inside and opens a faucet. Nothing. He reports his findings.

"Did you open the main valve?"

Artie answers with a look of helpless stupidity. "There should be a main valve somewhere just inside the house. You gotta open that before anything else will work. Lemme look for you."

The two men go inside and trace the exposed plumbing back to a place where it goes through the floor. There is a small trap door which Artie remembers, but has never understood its purpose. The city worker opens the door, and sure enough, there is a pipe heading toward the street and a valve handle.

"There it is. Just open it up and you should be in business."

Profuse thanks. *More than fifty years in this place. You'd think I'd know how to turn on the damn water.*

Artie kneels down. Mutters "here goes nothing" and opens the valve. There is the sound of moving water. Progress, civilization, clanking noises, moving water. Suddenly, the interior of the cottage is transformed into a fountain, with water spurting in a dozen directions. Artie stands dumbfounded, unable to make sense of the random streams of water going where water isn't intended to be. He becomes aware that the city worker is shouting at him. "TURN IT OFF! TURN IT

OFF!" Moving in slow motion, Artie turns off the valve to the water main.

The worker asks if he knows a plumber to call. Oh yeah, says Artie, trying to sound nonchalant. When the waterworks truck is safely out of earshot. Artie says:

Sonofabitch! SONOFABITCH! Sonofa-fucking-bitch!

For fifteen minutes he says "sonofabitch." He uses the full range of human vocalizations. Different volumes, different tones, different pitches, different accents. Same phrase. No swear words known to man sufficiently express how Artie feels at this moment. As he watches water dripping from every horizontal surface in the cottage, he has the feeling that maybe things can go downhill from here.

"So I say 'I gotta take a dump, wicked bad,' and turn around and walk into the house."

Cuzzin is standing on a stool, holding a propane torch on a section of pipe. He's clearly amused by Artie's account of his morning encounter, and chuckles intermittently between punctuations to request specific tools, materials, and/or beer.

"I take one of the most satisfying dumps of my life, but then I caught sight of myself in the mirror. Holy Jesus, no wonder she had a funny look on her face. I looked like the wild man of Indian Mound. My hair was sticking up all over the place. I had all this lint from the sleeping bag clinging to my beard. I scared myself."

Vroom-vroom-vroom-wroom. "Beer."

"I proceed to have the morning from hell, but then after lunch I see her out working in her garden. Here's an opportunity to make nice and to show her my cultured side. After all, I'm one of Indian Mound's proudest sons."

"Fuckin' right. Torch."

"I go over to the fence and say 'Hi Shawna'," because that's what I'm remembering her name to be, "I'm Artie. Are you putting in tomatoes? And she says, "It's May 2 and you can't plant tomatoes when there's still a chance of frost.' She doesn't say 'Moron,' but I can tell that's what she's thinking. Her tone is dripping with condescension. 'And my name is not Shawna.' But, of course, she doesn't tell me what her name is."

"Well, excuse me, Not-Shawna, but I only mention tomatoes, because the guy who used to live here took great pride in his tomatoes.' She gets this scrunched up, constipated look on her face, and says 'I guarantee he didn't plant them on May 2.'"

"Constipated." Vroom. "Solder." Vroom. "Beer."

"So I say 'We're not doing so well here, maybe we can start at the beginning. Hi, my name is Artie, and I'm going to be your neighbor for the summer.' She doesn't say a word but burns holes through me with her eyes. After about thirty seconds of silence I finally say "Do you have a problem with that? She says 'Yes I have a problem with that and a problem with you. My house means a lot to me. It's my island of sanctity in a busy world. There's only one problem with this house, and that's that it is next door to a shack, but at least until yesterday the shack kept to itself. Now, I look out onto a yard full of clutter. Some vagrant is helping himself to my water in the morning, and I have to endure some lunatic shouting obscenities all morning. This should make me happy?'"

"Jeez, Artie. You gotta understand the new people who live here are nuts when it comes to their houses. And for the prices they pay, they should be. Hand me the Saws-All." The conversation halts for as long as it takes for Cuzzin to saw through a length of pipe.

"I understand that. It doesn't give them the right to treat other people like dirt. Do you think she is acting this way because she knows about my movie?"

Cuzzin bulls his way through another piece of pipe, then hands the saw to Artie with a mutter of "Beer" and an open hand into which Artie places the can. "I don't want to disappoint you, but you're not a household word around here. People don't really know or care about your movie. My guess is that she just thinks you're a creep."

"I dunno. Among the feminists of America, I'm The Guy to hate these days."

"You're flattering yourself. So what did you say back?"

"I told her that my family had owned this place for a hundred years. That the cottage was completely adorable until my Mother died four years ago, and that I'm trying to bring it back to life."

"That sounds reasonable," says Cuzzin.

"Actually I was losing it, because then I followed that by saying if she didn't like it, she could shove her entire garden up her ass, and if she didn't like being called Shawna, she should tell me her name. She's pretty hot under the collar, too, and says 'Don't call me anything, just don't call me.' So I called her a bitch and walked away. Pretty mature, huh? And you know what happened later this afternoon--I heard every word of this--my agent sent me a UPS package. The UPS guy goes to her house and asks where he might find Arthur Gordon and she tells him 'He must be the old guy who lives in the shack out back.'"

"Ouch!

"'The old guy!' Who does she think she is?"

"The bitch."

"Yeah, the garden bitch."

"Yeah, the garden bitch of Indian Mound."

Cuzzin turned off his propane torch, took a swig of beer, and announced "Unless I've lost my touch, you now have real live running water. It also sounds like the battle of Indian Mound has begun."

Artie's to do list for May

- Call Elaine for update
- Contact Cuzzin & Liam
- Get electricity, gas, water turned on
- Fix plumbing
- Take old, crappy stuff to dump
- Wash bedding & towels
- Bomb house with paint
- Replace torn screens
- Paint floors
- Buy yardwork stuff
- Revive perennial garden
- Fix leaks in roof
- Buy an electric heater

Chapter 4 - The Depot

It rains during the night on Thursday. Artie finds at least five places where the roof leaks. One thing more on the to-do list. Five things more. When he looks out to the skyline, he sees a wall of gray. Boston Harbor is socked in. So is he. In a moment of intense loneliness, he calls his answering service to check his voice mail. There is a message from his son, Liam, saying that he will take the "T" and be at the Quincy station by 1 pm.

Good.

There are two messages from Meiko asking when she can come out to Boston and outlining in lurid detail the sexual favors she will perform for him upon arrival.

Good.

And there is a long message from his agent, Elaine Siegal, chronicling the latest events surrounding *My Mother, My Lover…*:

Artie, it's Elaine. Whoever said there's no such thing as bad PR never met you. I don't know if you are sticking to your pledge to boycott the media, communications technology, and the world in general, but if you're not, you should. Let's start with the best news. The National Organization of Women is willing to pay you $50,000 to be the keynote at their annual convention in Houston in August. That's $50,000 plus a bulletproof vest.

You didn't see Oprah Winfrey, I hope. She devoted an entire show to you. Rosie O'Donnell appeared as a guest wearing a t-shirt with your picture in a red circle with a line through it. I tell you, a woman her size shouldn't be getting on such a high horse. All the shit she's done, and she's saying this stuff about you.

Letterman's made that "Today's Dumb Ass" *feature into a nightly section. I called the producer to give it a rest, but he said that when people stop laughing, he'll stop featuring you.*

Wellesley College wants you as a commencement speaker, but I think they'll pull some stunt like giving you an honorary noose instead of a degree. I don't think so.

This will really frost you. You remember that nice boy from Esquire *who wrote that piece called* "ART As In Arthur?" *It was scheduled for the May issue, but they've pulled it and had him rewrite it with the title* "Arthur Gordon Just Doesn't Get It." *He was very apologetic, but I don't trust the little prick.*

There are a million requests for interviews and quotes, but I'm just telling everyone you're unavailable. I don't think anyone will try to track you down, but you can never be sure, so keep your head down and your sunglasses on.

I keep racking my brain as to how we can turn this publicity into a positive. Tell me what you think of this idea. What if you embraced your new evil role? You know, like one of those WWF wrestlers who is the bad guy and whose job it is to get the crowd united behind the good guy. Maybe you could say that's what you were trying to do all along with My Mother, My Lover… *to re-energize the movement for female equality. I'm not saying it will work, but think about it.*

By the way My Mother, My Lover… *is still doing well overseas. Box office is good and the critics think it's very funny and quintessentially American. I know it's not a comedy, but it never hurts to laugh. So I hope you're enjoying your little cabin. Let me know if you want some company, and I'll come visit. I promise it will be better than the* Sixty Minutes *party. Love ya, Artie!*

Sixty Minutes of Fame

Artie invited Elaine and about fifty friends to his house in Brentwood to watch *Sixty Minutes*. It was very early in the *My Mother, My Lover* controversy, back in the days when Artie thought damage control was still an option. Elaine had advised him to take the high road and not to respond to the critical attacks. As a result of his silence, however, everyone wanted to interview him.

When *Sixty Minutes* called to make their pitch, Mike Wallace, personally, told him he thought media people were rushing to judgement without even seeing the film. The press, in true sheep tradition, were focusing on the reactions to the movie, rather than the content of the film. No surprise there. Artie, in Wallace's opinion, had played the situation just right in refusing interviews. He was reminded of when Robert Bly's book *Iron John* was published. There was an initial hue and roar about it being the "bible of the men's movement" but Bly let the critics bluster themselves out then came out with a defense that had impeccable credibility. The academic community stampeded onto his bandwagon, and now the book is universally acknowledged as a classic work of scholarship.

"Ex-act-ly!" said Artie, thumping his hand on the desk. He immediately agreed to the interview, even though standard operating procedure was to let Elaine make the call on interviews. He explained to her that he had acted impetuously because FINALLY someone in the media was willing to look beneath the surface. Say what you will about ol' Mike Wallace, but at least he had been around long enough to recognize a media witch-hunt when he saw one. Plus, he had the clout and the *cojones* to be able to take the contrary stand. Let the critics peck away. The counterpunch was on its way, and it would be a knockout.

Wallace and the *Sixty Minutes* crew spent an entire day with

Artie. Everything was relaxed and casual. Wallace proved as affable in person as he had been on the phone. They took a walk around the grounds of Artie's house. They had lunch outside on the patio. They sat in the dark wood womb of Artie's library. The questions were softballs. The reporter asked Artie about film and reality, the state of the American culture, the changing roles of the sexes. Through his body language he encouraged extensive responses, letting Artie pontificate as if he was addressing a class of college film students. Artie could tell that Wallace was completely respectful and sympathetic, and that only his mantle of journalistic professionalism kept him from stating his agreement. He finished with:

"Final question, one word answer, do you respect women?"

Artie smiled broadly and comfortably. This, he knew, was Wallace's way of repaying him for a good interview. He removed his glasses so that there would be no barrier between him and the camera and said with warmth, confidence, and sincerity "Absolutely!"

"Thank you, film maker, writer, artist, and man, Arthur Gordon" said Wallace reaching over to give him a handshake. Arthur returned the thanks. After holding the pose for a few seconds, and hearing the call of "cut", Wallace leaned back and chuckled.

"I love that touch of taking your glasses off."

"You only gave me one word, so I had to make the most of it," said Artie.

"If I had given you a few more you probably would have said "Absolutely….. but only when their clothes are off." Wallace laughed heartily at his own humor.

"A little crude," thought Artie, but he laughed and repeated the punchline "Absolutely…. but only when their clothes are off.' Mike, you're terrible."

Wallace, continued "AND THEN ONLY FOR ABOUT TEN MINUTES!" And he laughed harder. Artie, relieved that his interview was over, and caught in the spirit of the moment, joined right in. Later it occurred to him that maybe he laughed a little too hard.

For the party, Artie served his signature poached whole salmon. He wasn't sure how this developed, but in Hollywood he was always known as a guy from "back East," and in his case this meant Harvard, Boston, and the sea. There was an irony to this., Despite the Brahmin images that were conjured up by the associations of coming from "back East", Artie came from a pretty ordinary family that had a modest cottage on Indian Mound which is a long way from Hyannisport, Kennebunkport, Nantucket, or Martha's Vineyard, but a short distance from Dorchester, South Boston, and Jamaica Plain.

The salmon *schtick* came from his former wife who came from a very social family that really knew how to throw parties. When she (she being "Evelyn") left him to run with the wolves in the desert, he worked hard to discover the caterers with whom she worked. Now, he could pull off the poached salmon routine as easily as going to the market for a bag of chips. Signature poached salmon was only a phone call away.

Spirits ran high. Many of the people invited were involved in the film and had indirectly felt Artie's pain. By the time *Sixty Minutes* came on, the martinis and champagne had been served, and everyone was ready for a triumph.

The lead-in for the piece was Wallace asking his closing question:

"Final question, one word answer, do you respect women?" Then, cut to Artie, squirming uncomfortably and stammering, the light glaring off his balding dome:

"Absolutely….. but only when their clothes are off."

Then, cut to Mike Wallace, his face a puddle of disgust with a single eyebrow arched in skeptical disdain.

Cut back to Artie, laughing too hard at Mike Wallace's "ten minutes" crack.

Fifty semi-drunk guests of Arthur Gordon, holding little plates of poached salmon and glasses of champagne, were paralyzed. Artie finally broke it by muting the television, dinging his glass and proclaiming:

"A toast! Here's a toast to the host.....who's toast."

Atherton

Liam Gordon balances himself by holding the overhead handle on the Red Line Train hurtling from South Station to the Quincy Station where his father was meeting him. A mini-disk player is clipped to his belt, filling his head with Bach's *Magnificat in D, Cantata 140* by the Orchestra of St. Luke's with Blanche Honegger Moyse conducting. In his left hand he holds *Come As You Are*, a biography of Nirvana. In other places the sight of a thin, spindly young man with armfuls of tattoos might draw attention, but in Boston with its hundreds of thousands of students, Liam does not warrant a second look from his fellow passengers.

In Liam's words:

I think "Hair Shirt" would be a good band name, but I think "Agenda" is perfect, because that's the problem with the world today. Everyone has their own fucking agenda and thinks that their issues are more important than the rest of the world" combined. You can have millions of starving children and people dying of AIDS, but if that sweater isn't available in the right size and right color at the mall, nothing else matters.

The other thing about "Agenda" is that "genda" is the how they pronounce "gender" around here and gender is the biggest issue of our time. I really think my Dad got it right in My Mother, My Lover... *and that's the main point of the movie. Too many of the "gender" special interests have an "agenda" which doesn't allow for anyone to present a view that is anything other than the one that is politically correct for the moment. My Dad, asshole that he is, is getting a raw deal with all the flak he's catching.*

I don't know how it's going to be hanging out in Indian Mound. He says the place needs a lot of work. To me it was always a place to play without being worried about the rest of the world. So I guess I'll see a lot of him this summer, which will be...... different. I don't know what to expect.

Meanwhile, it's nice to be going anyplace that isn't Dunkin' Donuts. I'm grateful to have a job and some pay, but I learned everything I needed to know to do that job in fifteen minutes! I can't imagine even making it there until classes begin, but I need to pay the rent. I know my Mom or my Dad would be glad to give me the money, but I like not having to ask them.

I know! "Hair Shirt" can be the name of our first album.
I also like the name "Lug Nuts."

Artie pulls up in the official company vehicle for Cuzzin's Bait & Tackle. He waves to Liam and the two embrace, a bit perfunctorily. Liam says "Nice Wheels."

"We're going to have great fun this afternoon.," says Artie, walking to the driver's side.

"Where are we going?"

"The Depot. Today we are going to be model American consumers."

"I'm going to be needing a little assistance," says Artie to a clerk wearing a nametag that identifies him as the departmental manager. His name is Atherton. The young man has red hair and glasses, and appears to be several years younger than Liam.

"I'm as good as it gets, at least at this store."

"Well, Mr. Atherton, let me tell you what we need."

"Atherton is my first name."

"That's an interesting name. What do they call you for short."

"Atherton."

"Is it a family name?"

"Yuh." He offers nothing more, but his focuses more intently on Artie. "Do I know you?"

"Impossible," says Artie, going into damage control and speaking more quickly, "Let me tell you what I need."

I've got this little cottage out on Squantum. It's a summer cottage, no heat, but it's very simple and very cute, adorable really. Problem is, it hasn't been well maintained, so the yard is kinda skuzzy and the flower gardens are overgrown and weedy. I'm not exactly a master gardener, so I can't articulate exactly what I need. I want to have flowers blooming and hummingbirds humming and butterflies everywhere .Most of my tools are shot, so I'll need them, too. Can you fix me up?

"What's your budget?" asked the red head.

"I dunno. What's it going to take?"

"To do it the The Depot way, about a thousand dollars."

"More than I would have guessed, but let's do it."

"That's what I thought you'd say. But who are you?"

"You've found me out. I'm Brad Pitt."

"No really. I feel like I've met you, but I can't figure where. Why don't you two grab some shopping carts and follow me."

First, let's think about the lawn. You need to make it grow, so let's grab some turf builder and a bag of lime. Before you apply it, you should aerate the soil with these spiked shoes .You'll also need a spreader, over there. Now, once the grass begins to grow--guess what?-- you're going to need to cut it. Grab one of those Lawn Boy mowers with the 3.5 Briggs

& Stratton. You'll need the grass catching attachment. Definitely a weed whacker, and I strongly recommend one of these leaf blowers to give everything that finished look. And you probably need a hedge trimmer Here's a gas can that you can use for all of them.

For the weeds, you can use this Weed-B-Gone Herbicide and one of these power applicators. You'll also want plenty of Miracle-Gro to get things looking good fast. A shovel, a hoe, a rake, gardening gloves, and hand tools. Let's give you one of each of these. There, just sit back and enjoy the flowers.

They are now at the checkout, with two giant shopping carts laden with bags, power tools, and equipment. The young manager stands by as the merchandise is scanned by the checkout clerk. The bill comes to $1053.91. Artie signs the charge card slip.

"Pretty good guess at the total, Atherton."

"Uh-huh, I'm pretty good at this stuff."

"You'll be seeing a lot of me this summer. I've got painting, roofing, screens. You name it and I've got to do it."

Atherton takes the lead cart and starts out toward the parking lot. Liam follows. Artie points them toward Cuzzin's truck. When they finish loading, Artie shakes the young man's hand.

"A pleasure, Mr. Gordon. And I want you to know that you've got a friend at The Depot and his name is Atherton. We're going to make sure that your cottage gets fixed up perfect this summer. And how about an autograph for me, too."

"Why would you want my autograph and how do you know my name?" asks Artie.

"Because I just saw your credit card and I know 'Arthur Gordon' is a famous movie director, whose most recent film is stirring up all kinds of controversy."

"I don't suppose you've seen it."

"No, but I saw a review of it on Channel 5."

"Was that the one by Cynthia," Artie stumbles on the last name."

"Yeah, Cynthia Tidwell-Kant. She didn't like it much, but I don't like her very much. So if she really hates something, then I figure it must be pretty good. You know what I call her?"

"I can guess." Artie is now behind the wheel and ignites the beast.

"Remember, Mr. Gordon, you've got a friend at The Depot."

"Well, friend," Artie reaches out and offers his hand once again, "You'll be doing me a favor if you don't tell people that I'm around. I'm trying to lay low for a while, and I'd hate to have the Cynthia Tidwell-Kants of the world trying to track me down."

Atherton beams, nearly snapping to attention. "Your secret is safe with me, Mr. Gordon. You've got a friend at The Depot who knows how to keep his mouth shut."

As they drive off, Atherton yells after them, "I hate David Letterman, too. And Rosie O'Donnell!"

Sixty Minutes made their segment with Artie their lead story, entitling it "The Great White Wail." After being churned and regurgitated by the CBS News editing room, Artie came across as a whiny, small-minded bigot, blaming women and minorities for his personal shortcomings. After every unflattering twitch or gesture, most of which were shot when Artie had a brief sneezing fit while eating lunch, the camera would cut to Mike Wallace's cocked and skeptical brow. Even Andy Rooney kicked the corpse by retelling the "Artie Gordon Jokes" cropping up on the Internet. With the ticking clock welling up in the background, Rooney smirked:

"Knock, knock."

"Who's there?"

"Artie."

"Artie-who?"

"Artie-who glad you're not Arthur Gordon?"

Liam, Meet the Garden Bitch

Liam's first job is to tune the spinet piano in the cottage living room. It's a job he thoroughly enjoys, as it brings back memories of staying at Indian Mound as a boy. Everyone in the family played at least a little piano. Maybe that's where his impetus to be a musician came from. It isn't a hard job, but the cottage is stuffy, so he works up a light sweat and removes his shirt. He goes outside to take a break, lighting a cigarette and wandering over to the Shea's perennial garden that borders their property. He is examining the new growth on a plant when she surprises him.

"Hey, get away from that *Nicotiana.*"

Startled, Liam takes a quick step back. "I was just looking at it."

"You were looking at it, and breathing tobacco smoke on it. Tobacco smoke is toxic and noxious to many plants. Just a little can kill them."

"I didn't mean to hurt anything-"

"I know you didn't," she interrupted, "but I couldn't let you blow smoke on any plants. You literally will kill them instantly." A natural silence followed, during which she examined all five feet, nine inches of Liam. Her expression could have spoken for her, but she was compelled to augment her disdain with words:

"Your mother must be so proud of you."

"Actually my Mom likes my tattoos."

"No, your mother says she likes your tattoos, because she loves you and doesn't want to hurt you. I guarantee she doesn't like them any more than she likes your smoking. If tobacco smoke will kill plants on contact, think of what it's doing to your lungs."

"Thank God you're not my Mother."

"I know I'm way of line saying this, but I see this self-muti-lation and self-destruction, and I can't help feeling the pain of a Mother somewhere. But why should I care?"

She leaves. Liam flicks his butt into her garden and goes inside. He finds his father lying on the floor in the breezeway, cleaning out an accumulation of leaves, acorns, and rodent nests from under the floorboards. He is filthy, but good-naturedly wallowing in the filth.

"Someday, Son" says Artie, pulling another handful of detritus from under the floor, "this will be all yours."

"I just met the neighbor," says Liam. "I just met the Garden Bitch."

Uncle Cuzzin

That night it is still too primitive for cooking, so Artie and Liam go to Anna's. Walking toward the front door, Artie hear Cuzzin's unmistakable laugh. "You're about to be re-acquaint-ed with your Uncle Cuzzin."

The evening is filled with food, fun, and fellowship. It is the first time that either Artie or Cuzzin has spent any time with the adult Liam. Ample portions of nostalgia are served, including lots of stories of working in the kitchen frying seafood under the tutelage of Seamus "Bull" Gordon. When the waitress comes by and says "Jizzwanna order, now?" Liam pronounces that he has discovered a new language, Squantese, in which Cuzzin is fluent.

By the end of the evening, Cuzzin, well into his cups, has turned the corner into sentiment.

I never got along with my old man, except in the kitchen during those summers. And that's because you couldn't question his authority there. The man was a genius. Kind of a cruel asshole to his kids, but a genius when it came to frying seafood. What made him special is that he was looking for perfection and coming pretty damn close The perfection he was striving for was simplicity itself. The fish or clams or scallops had to be fresh, and not just fresh, but tasting of the sea fresh. Even a detail like tartar sauce can be totally screwed up if you don't do it right. Tartar sauce is just mayonnaise, pickle relish, chopped onion, and pepper, but the ingredients have to be right. You can't use just any mayonnaise. The proportions have to be right; the utensils have to be right, and the process has to be right. If you don't refrigerate tartar sauce for at least two hours before serving it, it won't taste right. Did you taste the tartar sauce they served to night. The only thing wrong with it was everything. You know why, they take it pre-made out of a bottle. No one in this kitchen knows how to make real tartar sauce.

Liam takes note. The word in Squantese for "Tartar" was "Tahtah." Cuzzin continues:

Of course, Bull was responsible for the success of both Howard Johnson and Dunkin' Donuts. Yeah, I'm not shitting you. Howard Johnson was serving ice cream from a little stand down by Wollaston Beach. He was doing great, but his right arm was about falling off and come Labor Day, all his business went away. He was a regular at Bull's, always ordered the scallop basket.

It was Dad who told him that he had to get into the restaurant business. All these GIs home from the war. Everyone's buying cars and all prosperous. Highways were opening up the country. It was Bull who showed him how to fry a clam, and Bull who told him about the secret of cleaning the grease. And, when the restaurant was successful, it was Bull who suggested that he open up a second and that he make the menu exactly the same as the first. Then he told him "You should make it so that someone driving down the highway at sixty miles per hour can recognize your restaurant in one second. Something big, that really stands out. I don't care if you make the roof orange, just make it big and attention grabbing so people know they're going to get the exact same fried clams whether they're in Quincy or Dubuque."

Pretty soon there's an orange roof at every highway interchange in the country. "You better switch to sea clams" Bull tells Howard. "You can chop them up into little uniform bits of rubber."

"But they don't taste as good as whole clams," Howard says.

"Don't worry," Bull tells him. "People in Chicago or Kansas City wouldn't know a real clam if it bit 'em on the arse. What's important is that some pimply, sixteen year old kid in Denver can make the clams taste the same as some pimply, sixteen year old kid in Cincinnati."

"There was another guy hung out at Gordon's SeaFood. Guys'd hang out there just like they do at the bait shop today. This guy's running a little donut shop up on the Southern Artery that he calls the Open Kettle, and he comes in every Thursday and orders the fisherman's combo and onion rings. His name's Bill Rosenberg, and he's whining that his business is going nowhere.

"To begin with," Bull tells him, "your product stinks. You're making these lumps of dough that taste like they've been cooked in an open sewer more than an open kettle."

"They taste good when the fat is fresh," says Bill.

So Bull takes him out in the kitchen and shows him his filtering device. "Golly," says Bill. "Will you make one of those for me?" Sure, says Bull, but one more thing. Get a better name for your business. Something simple, but catchy. Something like Dunkin' Donuts.

The night in the cottage is unexceptional, meaning that it is marked by at least one critter incident. Liam goes to the kitchen to investigate a commotion and finds himself face to face with a giant white rat. He screams, a reaction not inappropriate upon the occasion of encountering a giant white rat in your house during the middle of the night. This isn't a little scream, or by any interpretation a muffled gasp. It is a bone-chilling wail that originates near Liam's coccyx, is powered by his lungs, and then is forced through the narrow channel of vocal chords that have been conditioned by years of rock and roll. This, in turn, draws Artie, who also starts screaming, through not nearly as effectively as his son. The men arm themselves with a broom and a mop and commence to shout and swat at the creature that responds by snarling and ambling away. When the house is secured they are back in bed, Artie notice the lights on in the Garden Bitch's home. They'll hear about this in the morning.

"What's in that bureau?" Artie and Liam are cleaning out the bathhouse, which means they are opening drawers that haven't been opened for years. Liam begins with the top drawer.

"Well, in the top drawer, there's a lot of mouse turds. Then, in the middle drawer, lots more mouse turds. And in the bottom drawer, oh, whole lot more mouse turds."

"Just what I've always wanted," says Artie, "a old bureau full of mouse turds."

"It's a family heirloom," says Liam.

"And someday this, too, will be yours."

"Howcome we're not millionaires?"

"What are you talking about?"

"Cuzzin's stories about how Uncle Bull was really the man responsible for the success of both Howard Johnson's and Dunkin' Donuts. Shouldn't some of that have filtered down to us, or at least him?"

"Um, let me think of how best to put this. I think the world of your Uncle Cuzzin, but he has this little problem with reality. My Uncle Bull had something to do with Howard Johnson and Dunkin' Donuts, but he was hardly the power behind the throne. Also, Cuzzin and his father never exchanged a civil word after the age of fourteen. Cuzzin never even went to his funeral. Tomorrow we'll hear about how Bull taught Ray Kroc how to make French fries. Let's just say time has healed a few wounds for your uncle."

"You know, 'Uncle Cousin' would be a pretty good band name.'"

Nucking Fuff

This is the day that Nucking Fuff Construction is formed. The inspiration comes when Liam is holding a piece of trim that Artie is trying to nail back onto the house. It's in an awkward position, and Artie is hardly a maestro of the hammer, so it's a success when the board is actually attached to the house. There's a one-inch gap between where it is and where it's supposed to be, but Artie deems it "Close-e-fucking-nough." Somehow this is morphed into Nucking Fuff Construction where "pretty close is close-e-fucking-nuff." As they work together, father and son begin to banter back and forth in the form of radio commercials.

Tired of high construction costs? Sick of quality craftsmanship? Here at Nucking Fuff Construction, we promise that your job, no matter how big or how small, will be completed in one day. That's our Nucking Fuff Guarantee. Any job, one day, it's done, you're history. Remember, we're Nucking Fuff, where pretty close is close-e-fucking-nough.

Doesn't it fry your ass to have to deal with plumbers, roofers, electricians, carpenters, and painters? Let's admit it, they're all overpaid prima donnas who whine about how busy they are. Here at Nucking Fuff, you deal directly with the big guys. We work fast; we work cheap; and we're not afraid to take the blame when we screw up.

We know what the competition says. 'Nucking Fuff is incompetent, Nucking Fuff has no stan-dards.' Well, now it's our turn. Of course, we're incompetent. Who else would promise to finish any given job in one day. But as for having no standards, nothing could be further from the truth. Here at Nucking Fuff we do have stan-dards. For instance, it's ok to paint over cobwebs and insects, but not over mammals. Or, for instance, when painting around a rug always try to overlap just a little bit, so it looks like you've painted the entire floor.

Officer Tropiano comes by in the afternoon. After check-ing on progress and explaining pleasantries, he says:

"Artie, there's been a complaint."

Artie, ably assisted by Liam, tells him about the giant white rat. Officer Tropiano can't help but laugh at the image of the two men thrashing about with their weapons of rat destruc-tion.

"Artie, what you're dealing with is a possum, not a rat. And you can deal with it with a gun, a trap, an exterminator, or a bazooka for all I care, but just do it quietly so the neighbors can sleep." It is so agreed.

That afternoon Artie buys a Hav-a-heart trap. Just after midnight they hear it spring. Father and son go out to the kitchen and find red eyes staring back at them. "Don't scream," whispers Liam. "Don't you scream," retorts Artie.

They have captured a possum.

"Omigod, look at the babies!" Clinging to the possum's

back are six little possums.

"What do we do now?" says Liam. Artie realizes he hasn't thought this one through.

"Let's put a blanket over the trap, and deal with it in the morning." The men sleep fitfully, interrupted by the rattle of mammal on steel.

In the morning Artie puts on leather work gloves, picks up the trap, blanket and all, and drives across town to the salt marsh near Germantown Flats where the possum mama and her babies wander nonchalantly into the tall grass. Back at the cottage Artie and Liam congratulate themselves on a job well done. Liam has to be at work at four o'clock, so Artie suggests they take a break from work and go for a walk on the mudflats.

Quincy Bay is like a saucer. The tide rises and falls on average about eight feet. Because the Bay is so shallow, at low tide the shoreline is exposed for several hundred yards out. The area beaches are ok, but don't compare to the open ocean beaches like Nantasket to the south and Crane's to the north. The mudflats, however, are a unique window into a world that is half ocean, half land. It may be just as interesting in other places, but at Indian Mound you can walk right out on the ocean floor and explore.

I've been walking these mudflats all of my life. Looking down at your feet is like reading the natural history of the Harbor. Look up and you see the story of humanity, the story of Boston. I know that sounds grandiose. Ok, it is grandiose, but hear me out. See this horseshoe crab? I actually know something about horseshoe crabs. They've been around in relatively the same shape and form for 450 million years. Yes, that is a long time. That's 200 million years before the dinosaurs were on earth. Man? Forgedaboudit! Homo Sapiens has been around less than a million years.

Now look up at the skyline. All those pretty buildings. You know how many of those were there when I was a little kid. Two! It's hard to conceive how ephemeral it all is.

But back to our friends, the horseshoe crabs. First of all, they're not really crabs. They are arthropods, more closely related to spiders and scorpions than true crabs. This is their mating season. The males come in first and then the women just a week or so later. It used to be just that way on Indian Mound. The men would come down to open up the cottages, drink beer, and get them ready for the season.

The highest tides are on the full moon and the new moon. The female lays her eggs and the males, attracted by the pheromones that she has released, are right there to fertilize them. The eggs gestate for the next two weeks, alternately warmed and cooled by the tides and the sun, and then hatch on the next flood tide.

It's really not that different for human beings. When you pick a mate, it won't be because you decided on it, it's because she smells good!

Of course, man is doing his level best to eradicate horseshoe crabs by so totally screwing up the habitat to make life impossible, even for creatures that have made it for the last 450 million years. This is despite the fact that scientists are finding all kinds of uses for a miracle substance called Chitin that's found in the shells of horseshoe crabs.

But maybe there's hope. This harbor had become a cesspool by the 1980s, but the water quality is somewhat better now. I've told you about digging clams here and fishing for flounder when I was a kid. You can't do that now, but maybe it will come back. Maybe we've actually learned a lesson, or maybe we've just transferred the problem somewhere else.

That night Artie hears a familiar disturbance in the kitchen. He gets up to a possum with six babies, looking disturbingly like the one he released earlier that day.

Artie tells his possum story to Cuzzin. His solution is to catch the possum in the Hav-A-Heart, then to take the cage

down to the waterfront and drown them all. It's real convenient, says Cuzzin, because everything stays right in the cage.

Artie tells his possum story to Officer Tropiano, who
offers to shoot the possum the next time it is caught. He
seems a little squeamish about killing the babies, however.

Artie tells his possum story to the Animal Rescue League,
but they rescue only cute puppies and adorable kitties.

Artie tells his possum story to South Shore Exterminators,
who say they will be glad to come over and lace his house with
rat poison.

Meanwhile the nightly visits have become regular and predictable. Artie spray paints a dot on the possum after he catches it again and leaves it off on Germantown Flats. The next
night it is back. So is the dot.

Artie attacks the lawn, and for several days the air is filled
with bits of grass, gas fumes, and the roar of a 3.5 Briggs &
Stratton. Through it all Shea sits contemplatively on her deck,
breathing deeply and repeating the mantra, "Endure. Endure.
Endure." Finally, there is a break in the two-cycle hue and roar,
and Shea comes to the property line.

"Arthur," she says calmly.

He looks up warily, prepared to go in any of several directions.

"It's a lovely evening. When you are done with the lawn,
would you like to join me for a gin and tonic on the deck?"

Artie is ready with an assortment of one-liners and come-
backs. None are appropriate to this situation. He nods.

Shea serves a cracklingly good gin and tonic. Artie tells her
so. There is a nanosecond of peace. Then Shea says, "Let me
be brutally honest. I don't like you. I don't like having you
here. We're completely different people who will never see

eye-to-eye, but you're here. You're not going away, so let's try communicating with each other."

Artie considers the proposal, takes another sip, and says "Ok, let's communicate. Why did you report us to the police the other night."

"There seemed to be some kind of domestic disturbance going on. I thought someone needed help."

"Someone did need help. Me! There was a giant, white, ugly rat in the house."

Shea laughed. "A possum?"

"Yes, but I didn't know that at the time. And the worst part is, he's still there, or I should say 'she' because there are six little possums clinging to her. And I don't know what to do." He recounted his litany of unacceptable solutions.

"I'm glad you didn't take any of those options. Have you tried talking to the possum?"

"The possum doesn't speak English, and I don't speak possum."

"I know it sounds crazy, but this is a frightened creature who's trying to look out for her family. There must be some level at which you can communicate."

"Talking to a possum? That'll be the day. It does sound crazy, and by golly, it's coming out of your mouth."

"Think of your options."

That night, instead of baiting the Hav-a-Heart trap, Artie puts the bait (a can of sardines) on top of the trap, leaving the entrance doors closed. When the midnight commotion begins, Artie approaches the kitchen slowly, without his customary broom in hand. The possum reacts with snarls and bare teeth, but Artie stands quietly on the opposite side of the room. Finally, the possum calms down and goes back to licking out the sardine can. Artie lets her finish before beginning.

I don't want to hurt you, but I can hurt you. I know you are a mother doing the best for your children, but coming back here is not the best for them, because if you do this again I will have to hurt you. I live here now and will be here for the next few months. After that you can live under the house, but not in the house, because it's my house. I'm going to open the back door for you and let you leave peacefully. For the next few days I will leave a can of sardines for you out by the edge of the marsh, but I don't want you back in the house again. I hope I've been completely clear.

Cuzzin's Recipe for Tahtah Sauce

Put 1¼ cup of mayonnaise into a medium-sized glass bowl. Use only Hellmann's Mayonnaise, or a rich commercial brand. Do not use Hellmann's Light, or for chrissakes, Miracle Whip. Shoot yourself instead.

Add ½ cup undrained dill pickle relish and ¼ cup finely chopped sweet onion, such as Vidalia. Do not use Bermuda onion or any yellow cooking onion.

Mix well. Cover bowl tightly with Saran Wrap and refrigerate for at least two hours. Will keep in refrigerator up to one week.

Part 2
The Battle of Indian Mound

Chapter 5 - The Rising Tide

Sandy Beach's Fishing Forecast for June

*The spring brings some of the strongest tides
and some of the best fishing. If you are a new-
comer to fly fishing, you will do well to spend
some time thinking about, and watching, the
tides.*

*There is no visible signal, no ringing of the
bell to the changing of the tides, but the fish know
when it happens and whet their appetites accord-
ingly. On the high tide, this works to the advantage of the bait fisherman, the chunkers, who
throw out a chunk of mackerel or pogie on a hook
and hope for the best.*

*The changing of the low tide, however,
belongs to the fly fisherman. If you have a
chance, observe the tide change before you actually fish it. Look for fish. Sometimes you can see
their tails as they dig through the mud, looking
for crabs, worms, or clams. Sometimes they
bulge the water from underneath. Sometimes they
make the surface "nervous." Sometimes it's the
baitfish who break the surface, chased by the bigger fish. Cruising fish will create a wake that is*

visible, especially if it's calm.

A good pair of polarized sunglasses will help, but there are also observation techniques that equal parts training and meditation. Let you eyes go out of focus and be aware of the perifery. Check the current, check the wind. Now wade, one step at a time. Small steps. Get your breathing aligned with your steps. Be aware of what is happening all around you. Gradually, you will become sensitized to anything that disturbs this wholeness. You will notice ghostly shadows as stripers pass over sandy bottoms. What you are looking for is something that doesn't belong in the picture. It's that simple.

Is it a fish or is it a dream? The only way to know for sure is to cast your fly.

From *Think Like a Fish* by Sandy Beach

1955

History has recorded little about Indian Mound. Native Americans of the Wompatuck tribe used it as a summer resort, a place to stay cool and to enjoy the bounty of the sea. They lived there barefoot and near naked, much as Artie remembers his own summers. Around Labor Day the tribe would pack up and head inland where there were more permanent structures and timber to use for fuel. Piles of clamshells, arrowheads, and a few human bones were discovered in the excavation of foundations.

As the English colonists arrived, the natives were pushed off into the hinterlands of the north and west, leaving The Mound to the seagulls and razor clams. For several generations it was part of the extensive estate owned by the descendants of John Adams and remained wild and undeveloped. When the farm was split up, the purchasers all had the same thought-to carve it into postage stamp-sized lots and sell them to the burgeoning masses spilling out of South Boston, the North End, and Dorchester.

Artie's father and uncle knew about Indian Mound from duck hunting expeditions. Even though you could see the venerable Custom House across the water (still can), Indian Mound still felt wild and free. A trip from South Boston, all seven miles of it, took the better part of a day. The last hundred yards were across the mudflats. At high tide you were shit out of luck.

The Gordon bothers and relatives bought a total of eight lots. They built themselves a little duck hunting camps, one of which became the cottage that Artie is currently trying to salvage. Within a decade there was a burgeoning village of these camps. The camps were painted into cottages. Flowers and shade trees were planted, and a community was born.

But this community was unique in that it focused around play. Indian Mound stood apart from the nearby neighborhoods of Hough's Neck, Wollaston, and Merrymount which were more straightforward extensions of the Boston sprawl. Because it was isolated by the ocean twice a day, you could put your workaday worries behind on the Mound. It was permissible, encouraged even, to be fanciful. Although the residents of the Mound were not wealthy, they adopted many of the trappings of the gentile. There was a celebration on the Fourth of July, with a costume parade, races, games, a bonfire, and potluck dinner to open the season. A corresponding one on Labor Day brought it to a close. Every Friday night brought an excuse for the Indian Mound residents to get together. There was an annual Lobster Dinner, a Bean Dinner, The Clambake, Gentleman's Dinner, and a Potluck. Wednesdays were for the Bridge tournament. Once a year the men played penny ante poker.

The Indian Mound Yacht Club was more tradition than a

reality. The men built a dock for launching the small sailboats that they raced Sunday afternoons and Tuesday evenings. The IMYC staged evening soirees with dancing on the beach and floating candle lanterns that bobbed romantically with the rhythm of the waves.

A Community House was built, complete with tennis court. This necessitated tennis tournaments, and a tennis ladder, and, subsequently, ferocious competition, Indian Mound-style. No one wore tennis whites or other trappings of the rich and privileged. Artie won a tournament for his age bracket playing barefoot and wearing the same bathing suit that he wore every day of the summer. Dead tennis balls were the rule more than the exception, as errant shots inevitably landed in the wet salt marsh. No matter, the balls were equally dead for both players.

At dawn and dusk an American flag was ceremonially raised and lowered at the flagpole on the waterfront. The honor of this chore was accorded to a young man of the age of passage (twelve or thirteen). Artie, Tubby, and Cuzzin had all had their summers as flag bearers. By the time Liam was twelve, the community had transformed, and the rituals of summer had disappeared.

Labor Day was bittersweet. After celebrating in the morning, everyone packed up and left at once, the time of departure determined by the tide. The sight of everyone walking barefoot across the mud flats, carrying suitcases and boxes, was both the sad end of a magical season and the promise of another.

That will look great on film. Longshots of hundreds of people all walking the same direction on the mud. Then, a fixed camera, about knee-high, as people walk by. How the hell are we going to lay a track on mud? Maybe we can get away with plywood.

Do the costuming up big-man wearing straw boaters and fanciful facial hair. (Maybe I'm getting confused with Victorian .Remember to fact check.) I see women in billowy dresses set against the sea. The overall impression is like a painting of Manet, or Monet or Renoir. One of those guys.

The causeway was built in 1955. Everyone was in favor of it. Unanimous. They'd be able to get to the Mound more easily. You could shoot down for a weekend or quick overnight in the spring or fall. You could commute to your job in Boston! In hindsight, you'd think someone would have resisted. You'd think a Cassandra would decry a future without a precious summer, where air conditioned homes and air conditioned cars mean climate-controlled life. Where kids would play video games at night instead of sitting by the sea wall counting shooting stars.

Growth and progress were accepted unconditionally in 1955. The first cottage was winterized in 1956. Before that, no human being had ever spent the winter on Indian Mound. By 1960 all but three of the cottages had become full-time homes. By 1975 Artie's was the last holdout.

By this time, however, Indian Mound had receded into the dim recesses of his past. He was in L.A. now. His folks retired and bought a condo in Florida, coming to the Mound each summer. When he visited, usually for only a day or two in between the demands of his new life as a fledgling film mogul, he spent most of the time bemoaning how built up everything had become. The cottage was the same, but the world around it had changed. To make matters worse, the water quality in Boston Harbor had deteriorated badly, attributable almost entirely to the human waste being dumped into the water via modern "sanitation plants." You could no longer eat the clams, and the beaches were routinely closed due to high coliform counts. The reason for this was simple. The suburbs were burgeoning and the population collectively needed to pee and poop. Not wanting to bear the responsibility for cleaning up after themselves, they did what human beings do with waste everywhere: they put it where they didn't have to deal with it. They dumped it in the ocean and let the tides deal with it, just as earlier they dumped it in the rivers to let it be carried to the ocean.

Simultaneously, the fisheries collapsed. Hough's Neck, the onetime "Flounder Fishing Capital of the World" suddenly came up empty. Everyone blamed the factory fishing ships that the Russians and Japanese operated offshore. These ships dragged the bottom, scraping up every living thing, then processing the fish right on board. Breeding stocks fell below minimum thresholds. Suddenly, there were no more fish. What few remained couldn't be eaten because of high mercury content. As with the clams, it was moot whether you couldn't eat the seafood because it was polluted, or because it was nonexistent.

With the construction of the causeway, the salt marsh no longer received a twice-daily soaking of salt water. The chemical balance of the wetland changed entirely. Within a few years strange new grasses were invading the salt hay that had been there for eons. In its place grew *Lythrum salicaria*, more commonly known as purple loosestrife, and ultimately referred to as the "purple plague." At first people were delighted at the colorful flowers, but eventually its devastating effect on surrounding plants and animals became apparent.

The causeway brought the automobile, and Indian Mound's three streets became jammed with cars. The long, thin playgrounds of Artie's memory became ribbon-shaped parking lots. The dust problem from the dirt roads was solved by paving in 1957. Great. The ensuing noise, clogging, and even speeding problems were worse than the dust. The arrival of cars also meant the end of the spectacle of bare-footed families carrying their belongings across mud flats on Labor Day. Now, there were days when the pavement was so hot that you could not walk to the beach barefoot. The days of the shoeless summer were over.

Boston Harbor, by the late 1970s was an open sewer. Artie still showed up occasionally to visit his parents or to drop off Liam for a stay with Grandma and Grandpa, but Maui and St. Barts were now where he wanted to be.

Perennials

Three weeks have passed, and the cottage has been possum-free. Artie thinks it's time to turn his energies towards the more civilized aspects of life, such as cosmetics.

Painting. That's simple enough. Buy a can of paint and a brush. Dip the brush in the paint and put the paint on the wall. Maybe to speed things up, use a roller. He goes back to visit his technical advisor, Atherton, his friend at The Depot.

"Have you prepped?"

Artie hesitates. He couldn't possibly be asking whether or not Artie had attended prep school. The hesitation is long enough to communicate confusion.

"Have you scraped and caulked?"

"Uh, no."

"Powerwashed?"

"Uh, no."

"And you say this is an old cottage?"

Atherton takes one of those "You are so stupid" breaths. "An old place is going to have lots of loose paint and accumulated grime. If you paint over it, things will look better for about a minute, but then it will all start flaking off. They key to successful painting is in the prep work."

"And what do I need to prep?" asks Artie.

"Lots of elbow grease. The old fashioned way is to scrape everything down, sand down the edges of the flaked parts, and fill any holes and gaps with caulk. More and more, however, people are using power washers. This justs directs a high powered water spray that blasts off loose paint and cleans the surface for the new paint. We rent them here."

"Can they be operated by a dummy? I'm referring to myself."

Atherton is taken aback by Artie's openness. "Just point and pull," he says.

Shea grimaces as her New Age mood music is overwhelmed by the staccato burst of the compressor. Artie points the wand at the cottage and attacks. For the rest of the morning it wounds like the Gulf War is taking place on Indian Mound. Shea goes inside, makes herself a cup of Valerian tea, put two *Argentum nitricum* under her tongue, and sits it a recliner, an eye pillow and headphone protecting her from the noise next door.

The power washer does a nifty job removing the grime and loose paint. It does an equally good job of removing loose shingles and tatters the screens on several windows. By the time he is finished, Artie has created several more days of work and given himself several new skills to learn.

"I think you've sold me defective paint. The wood just drinks it in and it looks like I haven't even painted. It's taking me forever, and it looks crappy." Artie is back with his friend at The Depot.

"And you're sure you've primed it?"

"Yes," Artie is somewhat indignant. "You're the one who rented me the power washer."

"You don't prime with a power washer, you prep."

"Priming and prepping are different?" He gets his answer from Atherton's expression which is asking, "How can someone who can direct a Hollywood film not know how to paint a cottage?

"You know what?" Atherton offers brightly. "You should consider spray painting. It'll go much faster, but it's a two person job."

"I knew you'd have the answer."

"Just bring your problems to your friend at The Depot. We're going to whip that cottage into shape if it takes all summer."

"And a million dollars," adds Artie.

Two days later, Artie and Liam have hauled all the furniture onto the front yard. They have masked off the windows with newspaper. They have donned their white protective body suits. They are good to go. Shea is back in her recliner with the ear phones and eye pillow. She takes a Melatonin, hoping that assisted sleep will help her survive the commotion.

It is late afternoon with the sound of the sprayer stops. The cottage has been bombed, inside and out, with white paint. Artie and Liam are covered with nearly as much paint as the cottage. Paint is everywhere, on the grass, on bushes, and the floor. Artie and Liam are chortling with joy at all they've accomplished. "Look at how much brighter it is," says an ebullient Artie. "And so clean," observes Liam.

Shea decides she can no longer live her life in a chair, and goes to practice deep breathing on the back deck.

Here at Nucking Fuff we finish all jobs in one day. That's right, one day guaranteed. We can make this guarantee because we are so damned efficient. Take painting, for instance. Some people complicate their lives by using different colors. Here at Nucking Fuff we use only white. Plus we use the latest technology, sprayers, powered by electricity. No more time-consuming cleaning of brushes and rollers. We just cover with plastic whatever doesn't need to be painted and let it fly. You'll be amazed at what can be covered in a single day.

The paint dries and Artie removes the masking. He is amazed to discover how un-thorough they were in their prepping effort. There is paint over dishes, appliances, windows, door knobs, light switches. The floor, once a slate grey, now is a Jackson Pollack of white footprints. Artie considers just leaving it as is, but ultimately decides to repaint the floors. It takes the rest of the week to recover from his one day of spray painting.

We don't cut corners as Nucking Fuff. We paint right over them. All work is done to our incredibly low but inconsistent standards. Forget to remove or cover the electrical outlet? Paint right over it! Doorknobs? They look good painted, plus they still work But it's best to wait until they dry. Windows can be painted shut, so here at Nucking Fuff, we don't go near windows with paint. At Nucking Fuff it's always close-e-fucking-nough.

Artie's major outside project is to recover what was once a perennial garden but is now a tangle of vines and weeds. He attacks the project the way he attacks everything--with every brand name turf builder, weed killer, and herbicide that The Depot carries. He becomes demonic whenever he starts the weed wacker. He is observed with amazement, amusement, and horror by Shea. Their disagreements have gradually become less barbed and less personal, but not less frequent.

"May I give you a lesson in gardening?" asks Shea politely after Artie has completed an epic frenzy of ejaculatory weed whacking. He is covered from head to toe with flecks of vegetative matter. Artie is frustrated enough at his lack of progress to throw the device into the salt marsh, so he is glad for the break.

"First, you don't accomplish anything by hacking the weeds into submission. They'll come right back. Instead, you need to sort out the plants that you do want from the plants that you don't want. Remove completely, roots and all, the plants that you don't want and compost them. Later, you can add the compost to the soil to bolster the organic matter."

"Whaddya mean?" Artie loads the chip onto his shoulder. After all, he is a Guy, and Guys know intuitively about lawn care. "This is going right over my head. I'm more of a technology kinda guy.

"Come over here." She waves Artie over to her compost bin. "I put all my raw green vegetable matter in here. I layer it so that it can breathe, and water it to help it decompose. The goal is the break it down to organic matter that can be returned to the soil. That's what it's all about-healthy soil. Healthy soil makes healthy plants, and healthy plants don't have bugs or blights or diseases. It all comes back to the soil."

Artie looks at Shea as if she is speaking in a foreign language. "Technology gives us Scott's Turf Builder, and Miracle Gro, and Ortho Weed B' Gone, and you say I should be sticking with rotten grass clippings? I put my grass clippings in that big, brown Depot Yard Waste Bag and leave it on the street for the trash collectors. I bought all this stuff. I'm going to use it. Man has dominion."

And, with a yank, the weed wacker whines back to life.

Shea's thoughts on dedicated tools: Forgive him, Mother Earth, for he knows not what he does. This guy has bought into the American dream, which is that "he who dies with the most toys wins." For guys the drug of choice is tools. They've got to have a separate device for every purpose. My favorite is the leaf blower. Now, there's a great invention. Tell me what a leaf blower can accomplish that a rake or broom can't do better and cheaper? I feel sorry for Artie. He doesn't even realize what a pawn he is in someone else's game. How can I get the message through to him without making him defensive or belligerent. He's such a dope!

Liam has a day off and comes down to be a member of Nucking Fuff. The cottage has been cleaned out to the point where people can actually start living there. Artie has invited Cuzzin down for dinner. His plans are simple enough-he is going to steam 4 pounds of clams, melt butter, and call it done. He has plenty of beer on ice. For hors d'oeuvres he serves potato chips.

Artie's to do list for June 6

- Call Elaine for update
- Take Liam to Red Sox
- Replace torn screens
- Paint floors
- Revive perennial garden
- Fix leaks in roof
- Invite Meiko for visit

Cuzzin's Inspiration

The Men - Cuzzin, Artie, and Liam - are sitting on the porch around a white, painted drop leaf table that frequently substitutes for the dining room table. Two candles provide the ambient light.

"Do you remember Sundays?" asks Cuzzin.

"Yes. I remember Tuesdays, too." says Artie.

On Sundays in the summer the Gordon clan gathered to feast. The banquets are impressive only in the memory of a child. Franks and beans and cole slaw and tomato aspic. The best feasts were when the men, including the little men, went out fishing and came back with a catch. Seamus had made up a special board that held the flounder so they didn't slip as they were filleted. Artie had impressed more than one date in his life with his ability to filet a whole fish, one of his few marketable skills. As the men deal with the guts and entrails, reliving the glories of their conquests, the women made things pretty and welcoming, catching up on the small events of everyone's lives, and the kids ran amok totally carefree.

"Do you know how many times I've heard this," groans Liam.

"I didn't realize it at the time, but that was as good as life gets."

Artie says "You mean I peaked at age 10?"

"We both did." says Cuzzin, with uncustomed assurance. "That was the high point of our lives, and we were totally oblivious to it."

"That's depressing," says Liam.

"Not really," says Cuzzin, "because there's always the hope of new peaks. What's been the high point of your life?"

The question silences Liam. He finally squeezes out "Going to Disney World?"

"Not good enough," retorts Cuzzin.

"When I got the Sega Play Station for Christmas?"

"What the hell's that?"

"A video game."

"Not good enough."

"Umm-m-m, seeing Pearl Jam in concert."

"Nope."

"My birthday party when I was eleven."

"Closer, but no cigar."

"I don't get what you're looking for."

Cuzzin leans back in his chair, and takes what can only be described as a long, thoughtful pull on his ubiquitous beer. "The best moments in life aren't the Hallmark moments, or the Hollywood moments, or God forbid, the TV sitcom moments. They're the ordinary moments that you take for granted."

"What's wrong with Disney World?"

"You poor, dumb fuck.. You've been watching commercials your entire life that have brainwashed you into giving that answer. That wasn't your answer. That was some guy on Madison Avenue's answer for you. Same with the video game, and the concert, and even the birthday. Those things aren't really your life so much as someone else telling you that that's what life should be all about."

"No offense, Uncle Cuzzin, but some of the linkages between what you say aren't exactly clear."

"That's exactly my point."

"What's exactly your point?"

Artie is at the stove. He has poured off mugs of steaming clam broth and placed them on the table. Melted butter, cut with a little broth and lemon juice, is set out in little bowls of blue willow. The steamers are in the colander. Artie shakes out three generous bowlfuls with a clatter and carries them to the table all at once. He makes one more quick trip to the kitchen to retrieve the cooking pot for the shells. Within seconds the rhythm of the balmy night is set by the rimshots of shells hitting the pot.

"This!" Cuzzin splits a clam, removes the neck sheath, and throws the shells and sheath into the pot with a satisfying clank. Holding the clam by the neck he dips it in the broth, then the butter, then plops it into his mouth, an errant drop or two of butter finding his chin.

"What?" persists Liam.

Cuzzin looks at him patiently, the way relatives do when they are helping a new generation transition to adulthood. "This is my point. It don't get no better'n this. A summer night, the porch, steamers, and the three of us."

"And don't forget beer," adds Artie.

"And beer," agrees Cuzzin.

"And so....?" Asks Liam.

"And so this is why the three of us are going into the restaurant business."

Fried Clams
-Random Thoughts from Cuzzin

Fried clams are really not the best way to express the art of frying. There are too many different textures from the rubbery neck to the bilious belly that explodes in your mouth. If you think too deeply about fried clams, or if you look at one too closely, you'll never put it in your mouth.

Another impediment to the perfect fried clam are the nooks and crannies. You're talking about something so complex that the female genitals are sometimes referred to as a "bearded clam," a reference that pays homage to no species.

I know of no place that shucks its own clams, simply because the labor is too great and the end product lacks uniformity. (That's why my Uncle Bull talked Howard Johnson into switching to minced sea clams, which are really like eating strips of unidentified fried matter.)

You want to start with fresh, medium-sized, whole-bellied clams. You can get them dry-

packed or wet in cans. Ipswich is famous for its clams, but almost everything these days come from the coast of Maine.

The biggest variables are the type of cooking oil and the breading mixture. I use the same mix for all of my seafood, but others prefer straight corn flour, now available in the Spanish food section of health food stores as Masa harina. If your clams are wet packed, just remove from the can, drain slightly and dredge with the corn flour. If you have dry packed, soak them in evaporated milk first, thence into the flour.

Serve hot on a paper plate or basket with wedge of lemon and Cuzzin's tartar sauce. The first fried clam is delicious, the second good, the third tolerable, but those thereafter represent the highway to gastric distress. There are simply too many places where breading can accumulate and grease is absorbed before cooking is complete.

One final observation. There is nothing more disgusting than a cold fried clam.

The Story of Shea

Shea does not speak with the broad "Bahwstun As" of Cuzzin or Officer Tropiano, even though she grew up less than ten miles away in the suburb of Braintree. She has the vaguely international polish to be expected of a public relations executive who attended the right schools (a graduate of Brown) and spent a semester in Florence as well as a high school stint as an exchange student in Brazil. She works in a steel and glass monolith at the public relations firm of Media Hub, visible across the water from Indian Mound, where she is a Senior Vice President.

Her primary client, until recently, was Banque Suisse, the parent company that recently bought out Beantown Bank. Shea managed press relations very ably during the acquisition, putting a positive spin on the fact that more than 300 jobs would be lost in the consolidation. Banque Suisse would be making Boston their North American headquarters. This, she pointed out time and time again to inquiring journalists, would enhance Boston's reputation as a Hub (she always made a point of using that word) of international commerce,. The long range benefits of this, she said with confidence, would far outweigh the temporary set back of losing a few jobs, most of them low-level jobs.

Everything was proceeding well. Everyone was happy. Media Hub was happy. Banque Suisse was happy. Shea was happy. Larry Cabot, her boss, was happy. And Richard (Ree-*shar*) Mobien (Mo-*byen*), Managing Director of Banque Suisse was happy.

Monsieur Mobien spoke five languages (French, German, Italian. Spanish, and English), dressed impeccably, and possessed the cosmopolitan self-assurance that Americans can only envy. His grooming was immaculate, his accent flawlessly Continental, and the twinkle in his eye when he smiled was beguiling. Larry Cabot, by contrast, seemed to be dressed in animal skins and carrying a club. Shea worked hand-in-glove with Mobien to prep him for the questions that would come to him at the press conference at which the merger was announced. It went off seamlessly. When one of the reporters asked Mobien to explain "in plain English" the benefits of the acquisition, he deftly offered to do it in "plain English, Spanish, Italian, German, or French."

Thus, it was a rude shock on the morning after the press conference when Richard Mobien cornered Shea on the express elevator enroute to the 72nd floor, pinned her to the wall, and began to fondle her breasts, trying to kiss her while reaching up her skirt to the top of her pantyhose. Shea fought back, but not before Mobien had forced his hand inside the waistband of her pantyhose and panties and forced a finger into her vagina. Her screams went unheard in the elevator shaft. When the doors opened onto the Banque Suisse reception area, Richard Mobien, looking as confident and urbane as ever, marched out nonchalantly. Shea, reduced to a puddle of sobs, rode the express elevator back to the first floor.

Shea immediately brought the situation to Larry Cabot, who didn't know whether to shit or go blind. He asked Shea if she was going to go to the police. She said that she wasn't inclined to. He asked her what she thought would be a satisfactory resolution, but rejected her demand that Mobien's testicles be brought to her in a Media Hub coffee cup. Finally, Cabot resolved that the issue was best handled one on one, *mano a mano*. Shea concurred. Cabot went to visit Mobien at the Banque Suisse office, and when he returned his relief was palpable.

"I think we've got this little problem taken care of."

What happened? Cabot beamed with the satisfaction of a man who has both protected his woman as well as covered his own ass.

"I got him to promise it will never happen again," said Cabot, beaming. "Not only to you, but anyone else. He gave me his word."

Shea is fifty one years old. She is 5'7" tall, with perfect posture. She is thin and angular, with broad shoulders and flaring hips. She's in great shape, very sinewy. Her breasts, in Artie's opinion, are about the right size, but slung a little too low.

In her Hub Media days she softened her straight lines with a flowing mane of brown hair that cost her $120 month to keep colored. After the Mobien incident, however, she mutilated her hair with kitchen shears, and now is letting it grow back in flecked with white. She's had the worst of her self-infliction fixed now, and her hair is a uniform two inches long.

Artie initially figures her for a dyke, especially in light of her hostility towards him.

Larry Cabot was completely unprepared for the firestorm that followed his declaration of victory. All he knew was that he didn't want police; he didn't want lawyers; he just wanted this whole thing to go away.

Shea is now on a six month leave of absence, with full pay and full benefits. She monitors email, but otherwise has nothing to do with Media Hub. Her days are extended exercises of yoga, t'ai chi, stretching, Pilates, meditation, gardening, reading, and cooking. The biggest thorn in her life is the new next door neighbor, but even he has become more of an amusing annoyance than a threat. At this time she does not think she will ever return to Media Hub. One day at a time.

It is just after eight on a soft morning. Shea has brought her cup of decaffeinated green tea onto her back deck and is beginning her morning stretching routine. She puts on a CD, very softly, of Tibetan chimes. The warmth of the tea, the sunlight filtering through the leaves of the oak tree, the chimes, her body.....it's all in harmony.

She is halfway into a sunrise salute when the rolling left hand bass run drifts over from the spinet piano in the cottage. Artie, who has been up for two hours already, is in the mood for Jerry Lee Lewis. "Well, come alonga baby, wholelottashakin' goin' on."

Shea is not. She finishes her exhale, then mutters a soft "gimmeabreak" to no one in particular. She tries to begin another exercise, but her concentration has been shattered. She goes to the railing of the deck and calls out, "Artie?" Again, a little louder, "Artie?" "Artie?" "Artie!" By the time she has appeared at the cottage door, she is lost on the other side of anger. Artie is just cruising into his final round of "Shake it baby, shakes!" Artie is roused from his rocking reverie by the sight and sound of a screaming woman at his front door:

ARTIE. SHUT THE FUCK UP! DON'T YOU KNOW IT'S EIGHT O'CLOCK IN THE FUCKING MORNING, AND SOME PEOPLE WOULD LIKE A LITTLE PEACE AND QUIET RATHER THAN HEARING YOU BELLOW LIKE A WOUNDED DOG. GIVE IT A REST, JUST GIVE IT A REST!

Artie, registering shock more than comprehension, stops. She slams the screen door behind her, and silence reigns at Indian Mound. Artie shakes his head and mutters:

"The bitch is back."

Cuzzin's Plan:

No, I'm not crazy and I'm not drunk. Well, no more than usual for this time of day. Here's the plan. We take the bait and tackle business and we restore it to its full glory as Gordon's SeaFood. We serve seafood and only seafood, and we serve it perfect! Lobster in the rough. Steamers. Fish & Chips. Cole Slaw, Onion Rings. The classics.

We take the parking lot and we turn it into an outdoor cooking area where we do the boiled seafood, and maybe even some grilling. You know, there's parking for more than seventy-five cars there. If we cut down those sumac trees in the back it will open it up to the salt marsh. We put a bunch of picnic tables back there and it will be almost like you're on the water.

It's all self-service, so we don't have to have a lot of help. It's simple. That's what's so beautiful. You can get seafood fried or boiled. You want Lazy Man's lobster, take a hike! You want a steak, take a hike. You want a baked potato, take a hike because we only have fried.

We'll make codfish cakes and clam chowda, and seafood chowda. What do you think about corn on the cob? Should we serve it? I also wonder about clam cakes. That's really a Rhode Island dish, you know, but

I can do them really well.

We don't have to tart up the inside, because it's basically an outdoor restaurant and take-out joint. People will come from all over, because this will be the best, the freshest seafood in Boston, in the world! We open in April and close in September. Go to Florida and go fishing. Five months on and seven months off. We can start right away and be ready for next spring. Liam can quit his job making donuts and help me with the renovations. He can stay here with you in the cottage.

For a sign I want to mount a giant fish on the roof. A striped bass, a stripah. I know we may not even serve striped bass, but that's the prettiest fish. That's what people think of when they think of seafood.

"I'm sorry about the noise this morning." Shea is sitting in an Adirondack chair with a glass of ice tea. Artie has approached the low hedge that separates their properties.

"And I'm sorry for the over-reaction."

"Sometime I'll give you a concert. I actually do a good Little Richard, too."

"OK, but not at 8 am. Had any possum problems lately?"

"No."

"Did you talk to him?"

"Her, actually. Yes, I did, but I have a hard time believing that talking to animals really works. That's the kind of thing my wife is into."

"I didn't know you were married."

"My ex-wife. My girlfriend is coming this weekend. You'll meet her."

What's For Dessert? The Dessert Debate, Part I

"You've got to have great desserts."

"Who eats desserts ?"

"Everyone. That's the main reason some people go out to eat, for dessert."

"Not me."

"That's because you have your desserts before and during dinner in the form of alcohol."

"That's unfair. I enjoy a good after dinner drink, too."

"You need something that complements the fried matter."

"I like brandy, and cognac."

"Like Key Lime Pie, or Boston Cream Pie."

"...and those single malt scotches, and weird stuff, too, like Sambuca."

"... or blueberry pie with wild, Maine blueberries. Or bread pudding. Or how about Indian Pudding ?"

"Maybe fried Indian Pudding."

"You've got to have great desserts."

(debate continues to rage on page 210)

Chapter 6 - Sandy Beach

Think Like a Fish-*The World is Flat*

One thing about Flats-they are never really flat. Outside flats are exposed to the open ocean. Their bottoms tend to be light and sandy, and scrubbed by the waves. Inside flats, which are protected by a land mass usually dark and muddy, and teeming with life. Whatever their composition, inside or outside, flats are great places to fish.

Flats are combinations of depressions, holes, ridges, and edges where they drop off to deep water. These are the favorite habitats of mussels and clams, and will often offer Eel grass, weed beds, rocks or other "structure" that offer great protection to fish. As opposed to most of the ocean floor, you can see a flat by visiting it at flat at low tide when it's bare of cover. This is the kind of intelligence that will pay off when you come back looking for game.

Large or small, all flats eventually drop off into deeper water. These edges may be a river channel "inside" or just deeper water "outside." In either case, this is where you will find the action-at the edge. The stripers will be at the edges when the tides change. They want to be the first over the flats with the rising tide to gobble up the clams, worms, and crabs that have adjust-

ed to terrestrial life. On the changing incoming tide, they will hang around to feed on the baitfish that have been trapped by the shore.

Combine the edges of the flat and the changing of the tide and the result will be action.

by Sandy Beach from *The Boston Globe*

Meiko

"How the frig did you do this?" Cuzzin is looking at an aluminum screen door. Artie is holding a rechargeable drill.

"I followed directions."

"Did you follow the directions that were in English?"

Cuzzin is trying to salvage a door that Artie has just finished installing.

"Jesus, Artie. As best I can tell you've got this thing installed upside down, inside out, and backwards."

"I tell ya, I'm good. To what do you attribute such rampant incompetence?"

"Low native intelligence. You're related to me, aren't you?" Vroom. Vroom.

"Plus, Liam helped me."

"That explains it. Runs in the family. How much did you pay for this thing?"

"$88 at The Depot. I could have bought it installed for $150."

"That's one of your worst decisions ever. How many hours do you have into it?"

"About six, not counting the time I spent trying to figure out the instructions?"

"It's going to be another six to fix it. I hope you fry fish better than you install doors."

"Whoa. I've told you. I haven't signed on to the restaurant idea yet."

"But you also haven't said no. You haven't run the other way. That's how most people react to my ideas."

"Something in my gut starts heaving when I think that fate has brought me back to Quincy to do what I did for a summer job when I was 15."

"I thought you were sick of that phony Hollywood bull-shit.. Could be worse. Oh, I forgot, it is worse! Every broad in America hates you, right?"

"All but one. Meiko should be arriving at Logan just about now. Liam's picking her up. You want to join us for dinner?"

"What are you having?"

"I'm grilling some lobsters."

Arthur Gordon's Grilled Lobsters

Get lobsters that are at least 1 ½ pounds. You must use hard shell lobsters, Maine coast lobsters. In general, by mid-July all you can get are shedders. Don't bother.

Light the grill. Use real hardwood charcoal (not briquets) and don't use any starter fluid.

Plunge the lobsters head first into boiling water. Don't become emotionally attached to the lobsters first, or killing them becomes more difficult. Boil vigorously for ten minutes (approximately half their normal cooking time).

Remove the lobsters. Crack the claws and split the tail. Place on grill, shell side down. Brush occasionally with lemon butter. Hand it in.

Please note: this is an inferior way to eat lobsters, as the best way is boiled or steamed. It is, however, festive, and a good change of pace.

Grease in their Veins

Liam at Logan: I couldn't feel more ridiculous. I'm standing here waiting for my Father's blond bimbo, who just happens to be Oriental, as were his last two girlfriends. And I like how he always refers to them as "Oriental." Why doesn't he just call them "generic Asians?"

Can't he see what a fool he's making of himself? Why can't he just buy a sports car for his mid-life crisis. At least I could borrow the sports car.

This family is so fucked up, and has been ever since Mom split. It's really bad for me to believe that the quality of her life is better in lesbo la-la land. Maybe Uncle Cuzzin will come over tonight so that all the Looney Tunes can be in the same place at the same time.

I like "Ragman" as a band name. It confronts the gender issue in an oblique way. With "man" in the name, there's no question where we stand on political correctness, especially if there are chicks in the band. "Ragchick," hm-m-m, that's not bad either.

But "Ragman" has the further benefit of double entendre, as in "What the fuck is your problem? Are you on the rag, man?" Then, there, the Biblical allusion to the story of the guy who gives new rags for old, and in so doing, takes on the suffering of others.

I will have to look that story up on the web. I seem to remember it having something to do with Easter.

Uh-oh, here she comes. Not hard to pick out of a crowd. Indian Mound has never seen anything like this.

Meiko is three years older than Liam. She is wearing a peach colored blouse, scooped low enough to show cleavage that turns heads in Boston even if it would scarcely draw a glance in L.A. Oh, it (they?) would draw a glance in L.A., too. She has the requisite tight designer jeans, $750 sunglasses, and beige platform shoes.

"Those will be perfect for the mudfats," says Liam, pointing to her feet.

"Liam?" She gives him a once over, a smile, and a hug. "You look nothing like your father? You're adorable!"

They chat at the baggage claim. She wants to know about his tattooes, and promises to show him the one on her butt. She asks him about his music and about the club scene in Boston. She's not stuck-up at all. Liam collects her two huge, green suitcases, and struggles to manage them to the parking lot. Meiko is stunned when he throws them into the bed of

Cuzzin's beat-up truck.

"Is this yours?" she asks.

"It's my Uncle Cuzzin's, but he's loaned it to us, 'cuz we're making so many trips to the landfill.

"Arthur Gordon is driving a beat-up pick-up truck?" says Meiko incredulously.

Liam fires it up and gives it a few throaty roars.

"I can't see your father driving this!"

"There will be a few things you might find different about my Dad. He's really into this handyman phase. He thinks he can fix anything, but usually he just makes it worse, and Uncle Cuzzin has to bail us out."

"While he's fixing things," says Meiko. "I plan to lie around on the beach, drink some pina coladas, and maybe hit some clubs in the evening. Are you up for that?"

"Could be," says Liam. "I'm not sure you're going to be able to pry my Father off of Indian Mound."

The Shortcut to China

Meiko's thoughts upon arriving at Indian Mound and being given a tour of the cottage:

"You've got to be shitting me. I can't believe people live like this. No heat, no air conditioning, mosquitoes, spiders, and cobwebs everywhere. The so-called beach has more seaweed, rocks, and crabshells than sand. The bathroom is disgusting. I think I'll get dirty even taking a shower there. This place is so ordinary! Artie talks about it like it's sacred ground, but it's just a shack.

Ah well, he seems to be enjoying himself, and it's really worked as a getaway from the media. Plus, Liam's cool, and I can put up with anything for four days......I think.

The grilled lobsters are a hit, although Cuzzin looks mortally offended when Meiko asks Artie to take the meat out of the shell for her.

"You can't do that!" he rasps. "You'll offend our ancestors. Here, let me show you how to do a lobster. Start with the mallet and smash the claws."

Cuzzin brings the mallet down with such force that the shell shatters and drops of lobster juice fly everywhere. Meiko gasps. The other men laugh, but Artie tries to ease himself between Mieko and Cuzzin.

"Relax, Cuzzin. Meiko's not used to this. Maybe she can watch me do hers this time, and she'll be ready to do her own next time."

"Get outta here!" Cuzzin protests. "Remember at the restaurant we said 'no lazy man's lobster.' That should go in spades for here. Really," he turns back to Meiko, "It's simple. After you smack the claw. You take one of these picks....."

"Leave it alone, Cuzzin!" There is an edge to Artie's voice to show the other man that he had infringed upon his protective territory. Cuzzin doesn't need a second hint. He turns his eyes to the heavens:

"Oh Seamus, Bruce, Mother, and all the former Indian Mounders looking down on us. Forgive my cousin, Arthur, because he is so blinded by pure, unadulterated lust that he is letting his manly hormones interfere with his seafood etiquette. I'm sure he will have his priorities straight by tomorrow." Cuzzin relieves the tension with his booming laugh.

"Well done," whispers Liam.

Meiko sits pleasantly through the lobster dinner. It's crude, but delicious, she admits. The conversation is dominated by Cuzzin, who regales everyone with the nuances of his sturdivant restaurant, despite Artie's constant reminders that he has not signed on to the venture. He tells her about Howard Johnson and Dunkin'Donuts. She's not impressed, even when he says the Gordon boys have "grease in their veins."

After the dinner clean-up is complete, Meiko nestles up to Artie and says "Would you like to go out to a club in town tonight?"

Artie is dumbstruck. The concepts of "club" and "in town" have never occurred to him at Indian Mound, although back in L.A. her request would have been entirely reasonable. When he finally collects himself, he is in full command of his graciousness. "I can't do the club thing here, Meiko. First of all, I've gotten into an early-to-bed, early-to-rise routine. But secondly, the types of people who hang out at clubs are the types who might recognize me. But what am I thinking? You're three hours ahead of us. There's no way you're going to be ready for bed when I am. You and Liam go out and have a good time. Liam, here's my credit card, and get the keys to the Lincoln from your Uncle."

She protests, but he insists.

The next morning Artie is on a step ladder, painting some trim in the back of the house. Shea is close by, watering her compost pile with a water wand. It's 11 am on a brilliant summery day that's bathed in sunshine. Artie has been working since 7 am.

"I've given some thought to what you told me about compost," says Artie to Shea. She looks up. "If compost is such magical stuff, why don't you shit in your own compost pile."

"Do you really want to see my bare behind hanging over this pile? But that's a better idea than dumping our waste in the Bay. Do you know that human beings are about the only animals that shit in their own drinking water?"

"No shit!" says Artie. "You know what I can't figure out. In the Fifties they built a pumping station out at the tip of Hough's Neck, supposedly to clean up the Bay, which was getting increasingly polluted. Instead, things just got worse and worse until the last few years when they closed down the pumping station and now the water is getting cleaner. Wassup wi'dat?"

"I know all about it, because my PR firm has had the Harbor Commission for a client for almost forty years. Originally, the western suburbs dumped their shit in rivers like the Charles and the Neponset, but they became polluted, so it was decided to pipeline the stuff directly to the ocean. Places like the pumping station on Nut Island were supposedly sanitizing the shit, but in reality they were just putting a little band-aid on the situation where more and more suburban shit was being pumped into the Bay."

"So, why are things cleaning up now?" Artie continues with his painting, Shea with her watering. Before she can answer, Liam stumbles out the backdoor. He is unshaven, with hair askew, and seems to be barely awake.

"I gotta go, I'm gonna be late for work."

"Did you guys have a good time?" asks Artie.

"Yeah we did, but we didn't get in until really late."

"How late?"

"After four. I gotta run. The donuts call."

"Need a lift?

"No, I'll catch a bus. See ya."

Artie looks at Shea. "I remember when I could do that. So, back to the shit." Shea continues:

"I'm actually a semi-expert on this. Do you want the full report or the executive summary?"

Just then, Meiko staggers out from the house. She, too, is bedraggled and askew, barely awake. And barely clothed in a bikini. She drags a chaise lounge into the sunlight, removes her bikini top and flops down with a moan.

"Your son is a very bad boy. He made me stay out until past my bedtime."

"Did you have a good time?" Meiko answers with an uplifted thumb.

"What time did you get in?" She answers with four fingers, then five.

"Where did you go?" No response. Artie, still on his step ladder, looks over to Shea, who has stopped her watering to take in the sight of the sleeping, bedraggled goddess in the chaise.

"Shea," he gestures with his brush to the chaise, "this is my friend, Meiko. Meiko, this is my neighbor, Shea." Shea smiles and gives a silent wave. Meiko is motionless.

Artie looks back to Shea. "Might as well give me the full report."

The first Boston sewer system was completed in 1884. Up until that time every community fended for itself. Now, however, the waste from eighteen cities and towns was consolidated in holding tanks on Moon Island, then released on the outgoing tide. The wastewater wasn't treated, just dispensed into the harbor.

Even though this was a state-of-the-art facility, the water quality steadily went down hill and by the 30s it was no longer safe to eat the shellfish taken from the harbor. Then, in 1940, three regional discharge plants were constructed. They were still simply releasing raw sewage.

The first actual treatment plant is the one you can see right across the bay, at Nut Island on Hough's Neck. It was completed in 1952. By this time, however, the treatment facilities were fighting a losing battle against the sheer volume increases coming from the expanding metropolitan area. By the 1970s the Harbor was a polluted mess.

Things just got worse in the 1980s when it was found that the wastewater in the Harbor was below federal standards. A court order mandated the construction of a new treatment plant which was built at Deer Island. Now all the effluent is pumped to the plant there, where it is fermented in these giant eggs that look as if they are right out of a James

Bond movie. The treated wastewater is then transported nine and a half miles through what's called the Outfall Tunnel where it's discharged into the waters of Massachusetts Bay.

The positive impact on water quality has been dramatic. Among other things, species of game fish such as striped bass have returned to the Harbor and created a small, but growing sportfishing business.

"You sound like a talking press release" says Artie.

"That was my job."

"You use the past tense," he observes.

"I'm taking a break from work at the moment, give myself a chance to figure out what I want to be when I grow up."

"Me, too," says Artie. "I call this my 'Northwest Passage' period, because I'm exploring different coves and waterways, looking for the shortcut to China."

"Which they never found," adds Shea.

"Which they never found."

Meiko is finally among the living by 2 pm. The day goes downhill from there. The skies cloud up in the afternoon and by late afternoon a steady mist is falling. Meiko spends most of the afternoon on her cell phone, telling her friends what a dump Artie's cottage is. They go to dinner at Anna's, but Meiko is less than impressed. After dinner she bemoans the lack of a television or other electronic entertainments. She makes more noise about wanting to go out to clubs in town. Artie resists and flatly declares that he won't go. She sulks so much that he finally calls Liam at Dunkin' Donuts to see if he will take her out when he gets off work at 11:30 pm. He agrees.

The next morning Meiko sleeps in again while Artie cleans out the crawl space under the house. It's a dirty, stinky, long-avoided job, especially on such a muggy, humid day. Why he saved such a filthy job for such a hot day is a question that he asks himself repeatedly. When Meiko arises, it is late afternoon. Artie looks like a swamp rat.

"Want to make love?" he asks mischievously. She sees no humor in the suggestion.

Artie suggests a walk on the beach. The tide, however, is dead low, so their walk is on the mud..

"This is GROSS. It's squishing between my toes! Ow-w-w! I just stepped on a sharp shell. I'm putting my sandals on. Oh crap, now my sandals are sticking to the mud. There are little things bumping into my toes!"

"Those are shrimp. Just like the shrimp you eat, only tiny. Relax, Meiko. Give it a chance!"

"OMIGOD! Artie, what is that?"

"It's horseshoe crab." Artie grabs the crab by its bony tail and lifts it in the air so that the legs are flailing towards Meiko. He's hoping for a squeal and a laugh. He gets a bloodcurdling scream. Meiko turns and runs stopping ever few feet to scream in pain or to curse Artie. He makes no attempt to stop her. After a minute, she had made it back to the sand and is running toward the seawall. Artie wonders if she will be there when he gets back. He gently places the horseshoe crab back in the mud. He is surrounded by the gentle lapping of little waves in a shallow bay.

There She Was

Artie is at peace with the world. Meiko's flight has liberated him.

In the distance, towards the Boston Skyline, Artie sees a solitary figure, moving purposefully, silhouetted against the pale blue of the Bay. It takes a few moments, but he finally registers that the person is fishing. He moves for a closer vantage.

He takes a seat on a dory that has been stranded by the high tide. He is no expert on fishing, but he has enough experience to recognize that the fisherman is fly fishing, standing knee-deep in the water just beyond the low tide mark. The graceful pantomime is backed by a big, fat, orange orb of a setting sun.

Artie is as confused as he is peaceful. He is entranced and mesmerized.

For the better part of the next hour he watches the ballet of fisherman presenting feathered lure. The performance is suddenly interrupted by the arch of the rod and a splash. Man and Nature have connected, and Nature is trying to escape. A small battle ensues, won by the fisherman, who lands and releases a modestly large fish.

The sun sets over the multi-colored gas tanks gas tanks in Dorchester. As the light ebbs, he watches as the fisherman reels in for a last time and starts walking back towards Artie, the shore, and civilization. As the man comes within earshot, Artie says "I feel a little like a voyeur, but I've been enjoying watching you for the last half hour or so."

The voice that answers is a woman's, "I don't mind being watched." She is now upon him.

"Umm, can I ask you a few questions?" A million questions are suddenly on Artie's mind.

The woman is now abreast. She is wearing a ballcap, sunglasses, a fishing vest with a million purposeful pockets, shorts and sandals. She takes off her glasses. Artie can't entirely see her in the twilight, but he can tell she gives him a welcoming smile. She has friendly eyes and freckles. "You can ask as many questions as you want between here and my truck." She gestures to the sea wall.

They walk fifty yards in silence. Suddenly, the questions come bubbling out of Artie as if he has been holding them in all his life:

"What exactly are you doing? Are there fish out there you can really catch on a fly rod? I know there are because I saw you catch one. What kind did you catch? Is it hard to do? Where can I get equipment? How can I learn how to do this?"

The woman laughs. It's a laugh like splashing water. Artie falls in love.

"Hold on, Buckaroo. I can only handle six or seven questions at a time. First of, what's your name?"

"I'm sorry. I'm Arthur Gordon. Artie. I have a little cottage over on Indian Mound."

"Ah, a member of the famous Gordon clan."

"You know us?"

"I know about Cuzzin of bait shop fame. I knew your Mother a little bit, a lovely lady, and I know about your Uncle Bull."

"What do you know about my Uncle Bull?" They have now reached the lady's vehicle, a small, neat pick-up truck. She breaks down her rod into two sections and places it in a rod holder mounted on the rear window.

"That without him Howard Johnson never would have gotten beyond selling ice cream cones on Wollaston Beach and Bill Rosenberg would be operating Dunkin' Donuts as a push-cart business up on the Southern Artery." She slips the suspenders off her shoulder, unties her boots, and nimbly steps out of her waders. She is wearing a faded green t-shirt and grey gym shorts. Artie, as a hard-wired male, can't help but taking note of her shapely, tanned legs. She tosses the waders in the back of the truck and reaches in for a pair of sandals.

"Do you know about me?" he asks.

"Not much. Haven't you been away for a long time?"

"Seems that way. Sometimes it seems like I've never been gone. What's your name?"

"Cassie." She reaches out and shakes his hand. Her grip is warm and comfortable. As much as can be communicated in a handshake is shared. "I can't stay to answer your questions, but you can get everything you need to get started at Cuzzin's." She opens the door, gets behind the wheel, and turns the ignition.

"It sounds as if you've been regaled with his version of the Gordon family role in fast-food history. Just one quick question. What kind of fish was that that you just caught?"

"A striped bass. About twenty inches long. They have to be thirty to be keepers."

"A striped bass. No kidding. I thought they were extinct or

something."

She smiled, but only with her mouth, no teeth. A smile that said "gotta go," and, suddenly, there she was:

Gone.

At the cottage, Meiko is in a froth of packing. She is doing it rather loudly, with lots of slammed doors and loud mutters. Shea is sitting on her back deck when Artie comes back. She can hear every word of what follows.

I'm outta here Artie. You bring me across country to sleep in a shack with spiders, mosquitoes, and godknowswhatelse.? You call this a cottage. It's not a cottage, it's a dump. You call that a beach? Beaches don't ooze between your toes. You seem to think I should be thanking you for showing me such a good time by letting me watch you paint. Then, for an excursion, you take me to the freakin' landfill! O, thank you, Bwana.

I'm going to the airport and catching the first plane back to L.A., and if you want to salvage this relationship, you'll be right behind me. Otherwise you can stay here and swill beer with your slob of a cousin and the two of you can smack each others' lobsters. I'm going back to the real world where beaches have sand on them, and you can play volleyball without risking your life.

I know the heat's been on you since your last movie, but at least in L.A. you are somebody. Even if people hated you, you were somebody. Here, you're just a little old man living in a dump of a house and driving a dump of a car. You better shape up, Artie!

Artie doesn't try to stop her. He doesn't argue or defend himself. He just calls her a cab. Then he calls Elaine Siegal,

"Hey, anything going on?" he asks.

"Not a lot," she says. "Mercifully. The press seems to have moved on to the next train wreck. How's your cabin? Do you want me to come out and visit you?"

"The cabin is good, at least by my standards. The roof doesn't leak, the plumbing works, and there are no more critters living in the house, unless you count ants and spiders. It's not the Beverly Hills Hilton, however."

"Maybe I won't come visit."

"I wouldn't recommend it. Meiko was just out for a weekend, and let's just say it didn't work out."

"How badly didn't it work out?"

"Badly enough that we need to do 'the drill.'"

"Ah," says Elaine, one syllable being all that's required when an agent and client have worked and grown together for more than twenty years. One syllable being all that's required when the agent and client have been through each other's childbirths, divorces, Elaine's breast cancer, and now Artie's career crisis. One syllable, when the agent realizes that 80% of her income comes from one client and the other 20% from other clients who she has because she has the 80% client.

"The full drill, or the partial drill?" she asks. Since the dissolution of his marriage Artie has been through a series of relationships, all of which have been short-lived and all of which ended badly. Especially since Artie has developed this thing for blond Orientals, half his age, the drills have been occurring regularly.

"I think we can get away with a 'partial'. She seemed upset when she left, but not apoplectic. Plus, Meiko's a nice girl."

"Even nice girls can get greedy when they think they have nothing to lose. You sure you don't want to go with the 'full?'" The major difference between the "full" and the "partial" is in the "full" Artie's phone numbers, email addresses, and post office boxes are changed. A restraining order is issued and 24/7 security is hired to watch Artie's home. In the "partial," the locks are changed on the house, and the woman, accompanied by a security guard is allowed to come back into Artie's home to get her possessions.

"No, I'm confident we can get away with a partial. Nothing else to report?"

"Just one thing," says Elaine, "The studio has announced July 1 as the release date for '*My Mother, My Lover...* on video and DVD."

"Well, ring-a-ding-ding! Mark your calendars, just in time for the holiday pyrotechnics. I can't be bothered with such minutia. I've got a fish to catch."

"You're going to go fishing?"

"Have I said something funny," Artie is suddenly defensive.

"You've said something hilarious. I cannot envision Arthur Gordon with a fishing pole."

"I'm going to catch a big, fucking striped bass, and I'm going to freeze it and Fedex it to you."

"Clean it first, will you? I don't do well with fish guts."

Sandy Beach, Salty Brine, and Rocky Bottom

The next morning Artie goes to Cuzzin's Bait & Tackle.

"I met a friend of yours," he says. "She told me I could learn everything I need to know about fly fishing for striped bass from you."

"You got that straight. Here's what I can tell you about fly fishing. If you are a pretentious elitist who wants to feel that you are some kind of snooty sportsman, then you are a good candidate for fly fishing. And if you have more money than common sense, then you are a good candidate for fly fishing. And if you never want to deal with anything remotely associated with actually catching a fish, then you are a good candidate for fly fishing." Cuzzin was so riled by his soliloquy that he had to get himself a beer. He slid a can to Artie, too.

"I guess I qualify. Except about that part about not catching fish. I do want to catch a fish. Do you sell the equipment?"

"Oh shit yeah. I'd be crazy not to. It's definitely becoming more popular."

"Can you tell me where to go and how to do it?"

"No, you need Sandy Beach for that." Cuzzin walks over to a bookself and hands a book to Artie. It's called *Think Like a Fish: A Fly Fisherman's Guide to Boston Harbor* by Sandy Beach. On the cover is an underwater shot of a striped bass with a green and white fly protruding from the hinged corner of its mouth. Artie turns the book over and reads aloud: "Tips, Techniques, and Secrets from the legendary Sandy Beach." Instead of an author's photo there is a familiar black and white caricature of a plumpish, middle-aged man wearing a yachting cap and smoking a pipe.

"Who the fuck is Sandy Beach and what makes him a legend?" asks Artie.

Sandy Beach does the fishing forecasts and writes a fishing column for the Globe. He seems to know every inch of the Harbor. He's also written some books on fishing. I sell them all here.

Beach is a legend to the fisherman around here, because he knows so damn much, but because he's been doing this forever. He started back in the Fifties and was rumored to be a fishing buddy of Ted Williams. The Globe in those days thought it was cute to give their writers clever names, so you had the boating news from Salty Brine and political commentary from Rocky Bottom. None of them stuck, except Sandy Beach. But if the guy in the illustration is supposed to be Sandy Beach, he'd be ancient today, but no one has ever met or seen Sandy Beach. So there's kind of this ongoing contest among the local fishermen to identify and expose Sandy Beach.

Wanna hear something funny? More than one person thinks that Sandy Beach is me. I know a lot about fishing, but I couldn't write a sentence, let alone a book. But I let them think maybe it's true. Hey, I can think like a fish. Can't I?

There's lotsa weird shit rumors about Beach. Some say he's old. Some say he's young. Some say he used to go fishing with Ted Williams on days when there were night games, but that would make him about 105.

Beach became big news a few years ago when he started to use his column to bitch about the water quality in Boston Harbor. I give the

sumbitch a lot of credit, because a lot of people felt the same way, includ-
ing me. Now that the water quality is improving, a lot of people credit
Sandy Beach for stirring the pot.

A few years ago he really started singing the praises of fly fishing,
especially for striped bass. Personally, I think fly fishing is for sissies and
pretentious phonies. Why fish with imitation bait when you can fish with
the honest-to-god real thing? I say it's pretentious because the people who
do it are all holier-than-thou when it comes to nature and the environ-
ment. They want things all natural, but when you tell them what could be
more natural than fishing for a fish with something that a fish really eats,
like a goddamn seaworm, they get all sniffly. Personally, I think it's
because they don't have a leg to stand on. Half of 'em that fly fish don't
give a shit about catching nothing anyway. They just want to look good
standing out there in the flats. But I will say that fly fisherman spend
money on their equipment, and I'm glad to sell it to them, so I shouldn't
complain.

So that's what I know about Sandy Beach. He's a fly fisherman, but
I don't hold it against him, because he knows his shit.

"Oh, Cuzzin, one more thing. Do you have a customer, a
fly fisher-person, a woman in, I'd guess, her mid-forties. She's
about 5'5", slender, fair complexion, nice smile....drives a
pick-up......she seems to know you......" Artie keeps looking
for the clue that makes the penny drop, but Cuzzin keeps
shaking his head.

"I'd remember a customer like that," says Cuzzin.

Chapter 7 - My Mother, My Lover, My Wife, and, now, My Sales Manager

Sandy Beach's Forecast for July

The cliché is that when the lazy, hazy days of summer arrive, the bass beat a retreat to deep water. That's not true, although their feeding habits do change. For the wading fisherman the early morning and late evening tides will be more productive. My theory on this is that it is not the feeding habits that change so much as the fish reacting to the heavier recreational use of the water. With motorboats pounding the surface and swimmings clamoring on the beaches, doesn't it seem reasonable that a wild creature will take a lower profile?

If you do fish the mid-day tides, try to access a place that doesn't have a lot of human intervention. This is a great time to fish some of the islands in Boston Harbor. This used to mean you needed access to a boat, but now the MDC operates ferry services to Georges, Bumpkin, Peddocks, and other harbor islands. Ferries leave from Hewitt's Cove in Hingham and Long Wharf downtown. This opens an entire new world of fishing so long as you don't mind being gawked at by the other travelers on the ferry. Bumpkin especially offers a variety of fishing conditions and is small enough that if one side isn't productive you can always walk to the other.

A word to the wise. Double check on the return ferry schedule. Miss the last one and you might spend a very uncomfortable night!

The islands fish much the same as everywhere else. Look for structure, mussel beds, and places that will offer or make available food. Where there's food, there's fish. The herring have just about disappeared, but the mackerel won't be far behind.

The water temperature is still several degrees below normal for this time of year. Look for the activity to heat up along with the water temperature.

-Sandy Beach, from *The Boston Globe*

Artie's to do list for July
> Call Elaine for update
> Buy fishing equipment
> Check out Sandy Beach
> Become world's leading expert on striper fishing
> Finish fixing up cottage

The Size of Your Dick

Message from Elaine on Artie's cell phone:

Artie, I'm glad you called. I actually have two pieces of good news for a change. First, "the drill" went off without a hitch. Meiko was a real lady about it. No hassle at all. Completely polite. I was surprised, very pleasantly so.

You're going to have to sit down for this next news. So July 1 they release My Mother, My Lover....on video and DVD. It shoots up to number 1 for both sales and rentals. We're trying to find out if it's a fluke or even, god forbid, a reporting error, but it's number fucking one!

Liam is visibly upset when Artie picks him up at the MBTA Station. He gets into Cuzzin's truck, and the two men ride back towards Indian Mound in silence. They're on the causeway when Liam finally speaks.

"I quit my job today."

"How come?"

"There are these two guys on my shift, both rednecks and both stupid. They keep calling me 'faggot.' Every time one of them opens his fucking mouth it's to make some comment about my supposed homosexuality."

"How do you handle it?" Artie is trying to maintain a calm demeanor. This is the closest he and Liam have been in ten years, and he doesn't want it to backfire.

"Mostly I ignore them, but it just doesn't stop. Today we were filling crème donuts. You can imagine what a field day they have with that. There are two lines and we always have an informal competition. My line lost by, like, half a donut to the other line operated by this girl, Cacia. These two guys are all over me about how I was beaten by a girl, and all. So I finally held up my fingers like this."

The car is now stopped in the driveway. Liam holds his thumb and forefinger about an inch apart. "She beat me by this much, just about the size of your dick!"

"What did he do?"

"Tried to hit me. Then all hell breaks loose. Donuts flying everywhere. Next thing I know we're in the supervisor's office. He wants to know what's going on, and I tell him I'm fed up with these two guys ragging on me and calling me 'faggot' and turning everything into a homosexual reference. 'Well,' the supervisor says-he's a fat Irish guy with a W.C. Fields nose-'Maybe if you don't want people calling you "faggot" you shouldn't dress and act like a fag.'"

Father and son sat looking at each other in the cab of the

truck. Liam is breathing deeply, still trapped in his own adrenaline. Artie waits for the breathing to slow imperceptibly, then holds a thumb and forefinger about an inch apart and says in a mock serious voice, "JUST ABOUT THE SIZE OF YOUR DICK.!" Instantly the cab is filled with the sounds of two men laughing.

Here at Nucking Fuff we have standards. No, we don't use the traditional tools of the carpenter. We don't even own a level or tape measure. Why own something you don't know how to use? But that doesn't mean we don't have standards. Need to move something a little bit, move it "a c-hair". A little farther," 2 c-hairs." Farther still, "just about the size of your dick." And farther still, "just about the size of MY dick." But don't be confused by the tech talk. Just come to Nucking Fuff, where all jobs are completed in one day and where"pretty close is close-a-fucking-nough."

They haven't been in the cottage more than a minute when Shea knocks at the door, holding a measuring cup. "Artie, I'm out of butter, and I'm baking cookies. Can I borrow some from you? I only need about that much." She holds her thumb and forefinger about an inch apart. She can't understand what is so funny.

Nucking Fuff Construction scrapes and spray paints porch furniture in the morning. When they are done, it looks as if they have spray painted the back lawn white. Artie tells Liam about Sandy Beach, and shows him the equipment that he's bought from Cuzzin.

"I've done a lot of reading and a little practicing, but I haven't actually gone down to the water yet," says Artie.

"What are we waiting for?" asks Liam.

"What are we waiting for?" says Artie, taking the question seriously. "Permission, I guess."

"Then I, as crown prince of the shabby cottage at Indian Mound, with the powers vested in me by the ancestors of the Gordon Clan, hereby grant the permission to go fishin'" says Liam.

I'll tell you what I know, but it's not a lot, because I've only been doing this for five days or so. You want to treat the rod as if it's an extension of your arm. Don't use a lot of wrist action. You don't need a lot of power. Let the rod do the work. If you can cast fifty feet you can cast far enough for most situations.

The important things, according to Sandy Beach, are to go to where there are fish. Present them with something that resembles what they are eating, and don't spook 'em. Sounds pretty easy. We know there should be fish here, because this is where I saw that woman land one the other night.

Striped bass like the changing of the tides for feeding. They like structure, that is, solid material on the bottom-rocks, pilings, moorings, wrecked cars, whatever. And they like places where they can trap baitfish, so inlets, estuaries, or narrow pockets can all be good. Here, you try.

Artie hands the rod to Liam. The tide is near dead low, and the Bay is as flat as a nickel.

"What's this fly?" asks Liam, looking at the feathered extravagance at the end of the monofilament leader.

"It's called a Whistler, and I don't know what it's supposed to be. Some kind of minnow. I only know that it cost $5 and Cuzzin tells me it's one of his most popular flies."

Liam flails about for several minutes, but with some coaching from Artie he finally begins to land the fly out reliably thirty feet away. On his third successful cast there is a swirl near his fly.

"Hey, I think I've got one!" says Liam. The line straightens and translates to a bend in the rod. Artie starts to yell instructions, but realizes he doesn't know what to yell. There's a moment of chaos, and the fly reel falls off the rod, into the water. Artie rushes over to help, but only makes the matter worse. Fishing line is everywhere. The rod jerks twice more, and then is still. The line goes slack.

"I've lost him."

"Maybe not, pull in your line. Maybe he's coming this way." Liam strips in the line. Not only is there no fish; there is no Whistler. Artie looks at the end of the line and sees the telltale curl of a knot that has come undone.

"Looks like I need to work on my knot tying," he says.

"Not to mention how to attach the reel to the rod."

"I'm just beginning," whines Artie.

"I know," says Liam. "What did that last two, three seconds?"

"About as long as your dick."

"This is weird. But I feel like I crossed over to the other side. Like there's life above the water and below the water, and through this divining rod we were able to establish connection."

"Well, for now, what's been established is that fish have dominion."

"Let's try again."

"I didn't bring another fly. You can add lack of preparation to my list of failures."

On the walk back to the beach, the talk turns from fish to women. Liam says he's sorry to hear that his father has split from Meiko, but not to worry. There must be blond Oriental women in Boston, too. Meiko caused a near riot at the clubs she had gone to with Liam. It was a heady experience to be with a woman lusted after by every man in the club, but in Liam's opinion, Artie is better off without her. The woman is living exclusively off her appearance, and Artie, in the humble opinion of his son, needs a real person.

"You mean I should date someone my own age? Never happen. That's disgusting."

Artie hopes his attempt at humor will mask his embarrassment at sober advice from such a whippersnapper. He manages a rueful smile, and says "Who was the rock star who said 'The best thing about getting older is that the young babes look just as good, but the old ones are looking a lot better.'"

"Yeah, and whoever said 'Hey Meiko, why don't you come to Indian Mound' had rocks in his head."

"Yet another woman who has Arthur Gordon at the top of her shit list."

"By the way," says Liam. "She called me."

"Meiko? What'd she want?"

"Just to say things are cool." Artie has enough paternal wisdom not to probe further.

Show Biz

The talk drifts to *My Mother, My Lover...* and the lingering stings from the public's reaction. Artie explains to Liam how his movie had its origins in the pain he felt after his wife left him just as he was coping with the death of his mother. Evelyn, Artie's wife and Liam's mother, accused Artie of having an affair with another woman. The other woman was never specified, because Evelyn knew enough about the world of Hollywood to know that everyone has affairs. The irony was that Artie was not having an affair with anyone. Evelyn was looking for a socially acceptable and financially secure way out of the relationship. What she really wanted was to turn her own life upside down.

"So she moved to New Mexico, moved into a home with six other women, and now works putting mud plasters on the walls of straw bale houses," he tells his son. "And as far as I can tell, she's completely happy without me."

Liam agrees that that is the case. He probes further. "That covers the 'Mother,' 'Lover,' and 'Wife' part of your film," says Liam, "but how about the 'Sales Manager'?"

"I could have added 'Lawyer' in there, because whenever there's a divorce, there's a lawyer close behind. I was represented by a woman lawyer who would rather have been running with the wolves in New Mexico with your Mother. There's nothing like paying someone $250 per hour to sympathize with your adversary. In fact, everyone I encountered had the attitude that 'of course, you're getting divorced and why shouldn't Evelyn follow her bliss?' I felt like the only person in America who felt that a marriage should be kept together.

"Anyway the 'Sales Manager' plot was stolen from a news story about a guy who was fired for sexual harassment when he hugged an employee, his female sales manager, who was distraught because she was broke, addicted to downers, divorced, and her teenage son had just run off with the family car."

"What happened?"

"In real life, or the movie?"

"Both."

"In real life the guy sued the company for wrongful dismissal, and they settled out of court. In the movie, the guy starts drinking, his life disintegrates. Eventually, he becomes homeless, and is set on fire while passed out on a park bench by a bunch of drunk teenagers, one of whom is the Sales Manager's runaway son, who has become this pathological predator. Meanwhile, the woman gets promoted, because the company wants to do everything possible to make her look like a superstar. The she has an affair with the Chairman of the Board and sleeps her way to the top of the corporate world.

"Maybe that was a little over-the-top," says Artie reflectively, "But hey, it's show biz. Did I tell you it's doing amazingly well in video sales and rentals?"

All is calm, all is...

Wide shot. Boston Skyline in the distance. Jets roaring overhead. Sunset turns to sunrise.

Military music, something with a snare drum, denotes that a quest has begun.

Solitary figure walking on mudflats. He is carrying a fly rod. Casting in different locations, different times of day. Taking the water temperature. Picking up a clam from the mud.

Music swells.

Interior. Reading in the living room of his cottage. Pantomiming casting. Now in the backyard, practicing casting. Casts into neighbor's garden, snaps off a flower blossom. Rocky-like.

Cut to neighbor, upset. Figure with fishing pole shrugs, smiles impishly.

Music gets louder.

Interior. Man trying to tie a fly in living room of cottage. His bungled creation looks unlike anything that could be found in nature.

Solitary man on mudflats. Manages to catch is own hat. Slips and falls. Catches boat on backcast.

Music swells. Single fish, silver with black stripes, underwater, sees man above surface flailing with fly rod .Ridiculous looking fly passes by nose of fish. Starts laughing. Second fish joins laughter. Entire school, a chorus of laughter.

Music ends. Freeze frame. Laughter continues.

Artie and Sandy Beach return from an afternoon of fishing. Well, metaphorically speaking. Sandy Beach has begun talking to him and the two routinely carry on conversations about stripers, about fishing, about life. Sandy Beach has become Artie's fishing buddy.

"What is the bumper sticker....a bad day fishing beats a good day at the office?" asks Artie.

"Something like that," answers Beach, "What did you learn today?"

"I learned that the strongest tides offer the best fishing, and that high barometric pressure is better than low."

"What about the wind?"

"There's nothing to the cliché that 'west is best and east is least,' but if there's too much wind from any direction the water becomes roiled, and the fish can't see your bait."

"That's right, and you can't see your own fly, not to mention how difficult it is to cast into a strong head wind. I'd give you an 'A' for the day."

"I've gotten a few 'A's in recent days, but still no fish," says Artie.

"Don't worry, you're gaining on 'em."

It's now mid-morning on a day that is shaping up as hot and muggy. Artie has been up since dawn. He made himself coffee, put on his waders over a bathing suit, grabbed his rod, and was out the door by 6:15. Low tide was at 8:32. He fished for two hours on the outgoing, then at dead low, took out his pen and notepad to make observations that would later be part of the log that Sandy Beach recommended he keep.

He is now several weeks into his quest to catch a striper. His results today are the same as previous days. He has been gone for nearly five hours. He fished the outgoing tide around Veasey Rocks, just off the western shore of Hough's Neck. Just after the slack tide, he thought he could see fish tailing just off the mussel beds. His casts, however, left him fifteen yards short of the fish. When he tried to wade nearer, he slipped on the seaweedy rocks and fell in with a grand splash. When he finally returned upright, his waders had filled and the fish were long gone, spooked by the thrashing of a clumsy homo sapiens.

Despite his failure, Artie feels successful. He actually found fish. He stalked them. Returning on the half mile walk over the mudflats to Indian Mound, carrying his rod and with his waders slung over his shoulder, salt water in his hair and wind and sun on his face, he is very much the warrior returning from the hunt. All is right with the world.

Turmoil

This is the moment you need to recognize in life. It's the one moment when you take a deep breath and feel a deep sense of relaxation. This is the moment just prior to life whacking you upside the head with a two-by-four.

This is the edge. This is where hot meets cold, fast meets slow, strong meets weak. This is where the action is heaviest in life just as in the harbor. This is where things are most interesting. This is the edge of civilization.

What comes next? Maybe it's the pain in the chest and the numbness in the left arm that tells you that life will never be the same. Maybe it's the phone call that begins, "Mr. Gordon? This is the Quincy Police. I'm afraid there's been an accident." Maybe it's your wife saying "Arthur, we have to talk."

Or maybe it's the moment you hear that damn ticking clock on Sixty Minutes and you see the teaser that lets you know that Mike Fucking Wallace is going to make a fool of you both on national television, but also right here in your living room filled with your best friends eating the poached salmon and drinking the champagne that you paid for.

When there is peace, turmoil can't be far behind.

Artie doesn't recognize the moment. He keeps walking with a little smile on his face until he looks up to the distant beach of Indian Mound.

Something's not right.

There is motion and movement just over the seawall that protects Indian Mound from the highest tides and the fiercest North Atlantic storms. There's also a new shape, a triangle that could almost be a teepee. There's commotion. Lots of people. Sounds, drums and a voice over a bullhorn, the flashing lights of a police car or emergency vehicle.

The tableau only becomes more absurd as it comes into sharper focus. There are Indians, Native Americans, maybe twenty of them, in full war paint, beating drums, chanting, and carrying signs that read "Indian Mound is Our Home" and "We Sold You Manhattan, But Not The Mound" and "Give us Back Our Sacred Ground."

Artie says to himself. "I get it, someone's making a movie." And there are cameras, but not for making a film. These are cameras for television. As he mounts the cement steps over the seawall, he can see what appears to be the entire population of Indian Mound milling about. Artie walks over to the police car, beacon flashing, where Tubby Tropiano is standing in full uniform.

"What is this?" asks Artie. He is actually feeling amusement at the unexpected spectacle.

"This is bullshit is what it is." There is no amusement in Tubby's voice, nor in his posture. He spits out each word with dry bile. "I'm here to protect these fucking dirtbags while they're try to steal my home. This is bullshit!"

"Who are these people?"

"They're fucking crooks pretending to be Indians. Oh, excuse me, Native Americans. And they want us to give them our houses so they can build a casino and sell tax free cigarettes. This is fucking bullshit, and it's my job to fucking protect them. Well, they better know that there comes a time when I get off duty."

Artie leaves Tubby to his mutters, and walks over to where a small semi-circle of Mounders are gathered around a Channel 5 news camera that is pointed at a smartly dressed young woman holding a microphone. She is looking extremely self-conscious. Just to her right is a young man with shoulder-length dark hair and a painted face. He is wearing a cordless headset and is speaking apparently to no one.

"I'm just about to do Channel 5. Everybody's here. *The Globe, The Herald,* and the *Monitor* all sent reporters. Good work! We might even get a feed to the networks. Yeah, they're sputtering about as expected. Ugly, but not violent."

He gives a quick laugh. "Spewing might be a better description."

"Ready when you are, Heather" says the man operating the camera. The woman tilts her microphone towards the young man, who mutters a quick "gotta go" and removes his headset and clips it to his belt. Immediately another painted man, carrying a feathered headress, steps forward and puts it on the first man from behind, who sidesteps to the woman with the microphone. After a quick preening, he gives the woman a slight nod, who passes it along to the cameraman. They've done this before.

"A-a-an-n-nd, rolling."

Heather: *I'm here at the quiet seaside village of Indian Mound, which is anything but quiet today. You can probably hear the drums in the background. The Wompanoag Tribe is claiming that this is a sacred burial site for their tribe that was wrongly taken from them when colonial settlers broke their treaty with the Wompanoags back in 1725. And, as you might imagine, local residents are none too happy about it.*

As if on cue, the people watching the interview start shouting and booing, sputtering and spewing. Artie realizes, they are on cue.

With me is tribal spokesperson, Joe Liquordup. First of all, is that your real name?

Joe: *It's not my given name, but it's my real name. I took it when I realized how systematically my people have been suppressed and exploited since the English colonists arrived. Our lands have been stolen, our access to resources denied, and as a people we've been shackled and sedated. I chose this name so the white man could see that I've confronted my demons and am now ready to ask for what rightfully belongs to my people.*

Heather: *But why Indian Mound?*

Joe: *Because we're reasonable and responsible people. We could say "Give us back Massachusetts, but this is the 21st century. Indian Mound is where our people came to enjoy the good life. We hunted and fished and gathered clams here. We also buried our dead here. If at least our sacred spaces are returned to us, then something meaningful will have been done to right the wrongs of the last three centuries.*

Heather: *Do you expect these people to give you their homes?*

Joe: *Not without compensation. We have nothing against these people. They didn't take our sacred spaces, but their ancestors did. All we're asking is Wompanoags be treated fairly, and we're not going to be ignored, marginalized, or trivialized. That's why we are staying here until Indian Mound is returned to us.*

Heather: *How are you prepared to compensate them?*

Joe: *I didn't say we would compensate them, only that they should be compensated. We're not the ones who broke the treaty. We shouldn't have to make reparations.*

Heather: *That's the Wompanoag position, but as you might imagine, there's another side to the story.*

She smiles and freezes.

"A-a-an-n-nd, cut," says the cameraman. Joe and Heather

exchange a brief nod. His assistant removes his headdress, and he immediately replaces it with his headset. Within seconds he is talking purposefully into space.

Heather meanwhile has replaced Joe with a man that Artie recognizes as being from Indian Mound. He is overweight, with a red face. He has the Irish face, handsome in youth, but now puffed with anger and disappointment. After a few moments of conversation that Artie can't hear, the interview rituals are repeated:

Heather: *With me is Dennis McGuinty, one of the Indian Mound residents who will be displaced if the Wompanoags have their way. What do you think of the Wompanoag claim that Indian Mound is a sacred burial site?*

In contrast to Liquordup who was relaxed and articulate, obviously comfortable with the interviewing process, McGuinty is agitated. He leans over and gets much too close to the microphone:

Dennis: *I think it's bullshit!*

Heather drops the microphone. The camera operator yells "cut," and Heather tells Dennis they can't use that word on the air. "Let's approach this a different way," she suggests.

Heather: *With me is Dennis McGuinty, one of the Indian Mound residents who will be displaced if the Wompanoags have their way. How long have you lived here?*

Dennis: *Fowa yiz, and I ain't plannin' t'leave soon.*

He speaks fluent Squantese.

Heather: *Do you own a home here?*

Dennis: *Yuh, we bought our place for a hunnert 'n twenny-five gran and musta put another thirty-fawty int'it. I ain gonna handit ovah to someone pretendin' to be an Indyin who wantsta build a cahsino.*

Heather: *Have you ever heard that this is a sacred Indian Burial site?*

Dennis looks at her, exasperated. He pauses:

Dennis: *I tellya it's pyuwah bullshit.*
Heather drops the mic again and says "We can go with what we've got."

Artie hangs around the waterfront for another hour, watching various sideshows. The Indians erect another teepee. There are more interviews. At one point a shouting match breaks out between Kathleen, Tubby Tropiano's wife, and one of the Native Americans. Actually, it's not a "match" because it only involves Kathleen screaming obscenitites.
Artie is just preparing to go home when Shea approaches him.
"There's going to be a meeting of Indian Mound residents tonight down on the site of the old community house. I guess that includes you. Seven thirty, bring a lawn chair."

The Test Kitchen is Now Operational

"The test kitchen is now in operation." Cuzzin and Artie are seated on lawn chairs, along with the other residents of Indian Mound. They are crowded into McGuinty's back yard, focused around McGuinty's deck.
"What the hell are you talking about?" asks Artie.
"I've set up a test kitchen for the restaurant. I bought little

commercial grade fryer, and I'm going to re-teach myself how to cook fish & chips, fried clams, French fries, rings, all the good stuff. You gotta come up and let me show you the plan."

"Are you serious?"

"You've never known me to be so serious. Are you in or out?"

"Jeez Cuzzin. I don't know. I've expected this whole restaurant thing to blow over. To tell you the truth I'm so concerned about my own shit. I haven't given it any thought." Artie looked at his cousin. Cuzzin did his best to look back with a glint of determination. There was a pause:

"How do you like my glint of determination?" asks Cuzzin steadily. Vroom-vroom-vroom. "Just come by the shop sometime. I'll fry up some sea worms for you."

"Who's that guy who looks like Peewee Herman?" asks Artie. He motions to a slight man, balding, with glasses who is standing in front of the assembled residents, ineffectively calling for attention. As soon as he makes the connection. Cuzzin starts laughing.

"Jeez, he does look like Peewee. It's Jerry Sweeney. He's a mouthpiece." The crowd has finally quieted.

"Hi, thanks for coming, although I know most of us would have preferred to be at home watching the Red Sox. Wouldn't you know it? They're playing the Indians tonight." Sweeney pauses. No one laughs. He continues, "A couple of you asked me to run this meeting. I guess because I'm a lawyer, although I'm a tax specialist so this is way out of my league, although it is a taxing situation."

No one laughs again.

"So, one way to get started is for us just to express what's on our minds and to let others react. I'll begin by saying, personally, I think this is a very serious situation and that we should get ourselves the best legal counsel we can afford. I'm talking about a $300 dollar an hour type. Some guy from one of the big firms in town where they've got really deep resources to pull from. Uh, Mike, go ahead."

Mike del Vecchio, an Italian version of Dennis McGuinty. "Why can't we just tell them to get the hell outta here? If a bunch of teenagers camped on the beach, we'd have 'em outta here in a minute."

Suddenly, everyone is speaking:

"There must be health department regulations. Where are they going to go to the bathroom?"

"They're working in shifts. The teepees will be occupied 24/7, but every three/four hours, new people come."

"Some Indians. They all have cell phones and those personal data things."

"I heard this happened to a town in Maine. People couldn't sell their houses after the Indians claimed the land."

"Waitaminute! Hold on everybody! Order! Order!" Sweeney was trying, without success, to regain control of the crowd. Just as chaos was about to reign, Cuzzin bailed him out with an ear-splitting whistle.

"That's better, thank you. Now people, I think we will all agree that the only way we're going to have a productive meeting is if we all agree that only one person speaks at a time. Are we all agreed? Good. Now, the floor recognizes Clarence."

Artie and Cuzzin looked at each other. "Clarence" was the reason why Tubby tolerated his nickname.

"What they're doing breaks about fifty statutes, but we've got orders right from the Mayor. Let them stay, and make sure no one harms the sonsabitches. That's why you see the squad car down there."

"Why's the Mayor on their side?" asks Sweeney.

"He's not," says Tubby, "but he's a politician and politicians know that it's very politically incorrect to come down on Native Americans these days. He knows that every single guy on the police force thinks this is bullshit, but he's telling us to live with it, until things can be sorted out."

"OK, thank you," says Sweeney deferentially. "Now, Shea."

Shea stands. She's composed, casual. She's wearing a yoke-necked aqua top and off-white, linen slacks.

She's wearing make-up, Artie realizes. She looks good.

"We're fighting a battle on two entirely different fronts. We keep jumping from one to the other. As a result we're appearing confused and disorganized. The first is the legal front. None of knows where we stand. Aside from Sweeney, none of us are lawyers, and even he admits he doesn't begin to understand the real issues here. The second front is public relations, the proverbial court of public opinion. This is an area where we should be able to hold our own, but I gotta tell you, the Indians won the opening battle decisively this afternoon."

"Didja see the coverage on Channel 5?"

"That Indian guy is such a fake, wearing that headdress."

"No one should let Dennis near a microphone again."

"It's bullshit, and we all know it. I just said it."

It took another blast from Cuzzin to return the floor to Shea:

"Dennis did his best, but we're up against media-savvy pros. They know how to present themselves while we're all emotionally caught up in the moment. Anger is not a helpful emotion in a situation like this. I feel strongly that we should designate a single spokesperson to talk to the media. Someone cool and calm, who can present the interests of the residents without making us seem like a bunch of redneck racists."

"But we are redneck racists," blurted Cuzzin, generating a few hoots of support. "Especially when it comes to protecting out homes."

Shea looks through him. With a professional mask of disinterest on her face Artie recognizes that she is already in character. "And we should meet nightly, discuss the events of the day, bring forward new information, and, if necessary, adjust our community position that the spokesperson presents the outside world."

"I don't know if we need to create a procedure," says Sweeney, "but I nominate you." This was followed by a lot of yeah-yeah-yeahs.

"I'll be glad to do it," says Shea.

"In that case," inserts Sweeney. "We don't even have to vote. You're elected, and you might as well run the meeting, too." This, too, is met with concensus. Shea replaces Sweeney, who gratefully slips back into the anonymity of the crowd.

"OK, who's next?" says Shea.

Artie raises his hand.

For those of you who don't know me, I'm Arthur Gordon. My family has owned property on Indian Mound for over 100 years, and I'm currently living in the only remaining summer cottage. I bring a slightly detached viewpoint, since I don't live here full-time. What I'd like to urge is for everyone to take a deep breath and try to look at the situation with less emotion. I heard a million rumors today, most of them ridiculous. For instance, there's no possibility of building a casino here. You couldn't even fit the employee parking lot for a casino on Indian Mound. So, you have to ask yourself "What do these people want? Why are they doing this?" because until you can see things through the other guy's eyes, you don't know what or how to negotiate.

There was one second of silence before the tsunami of hostility. If Artie had been trying to coalesce the group to united action, he succeeded magnificently:

"Easy for you to say. You've got nothing to lose."

"Who asked you, anyway?"

"You don't own a house here, you own a shack."

"I'd give your place to the redskins, but they wouldn't take it."

"How do you make nice to someone who's trying to steal your home?"

"Your shack is holding down the values of the rest of our properties."

"Why should we kiss their red asses?"

"The only good Indian is a dead Indian."

"The rest of us live in real houses. You live in an eyesore."

Cuzzin whistles. Shea gets the meeting back under control. Shea says there is always wisdom to seeing the opposing view, but Artie doesn't hear anything more. He descends into a bubbling stew of fuming obsession. Fuck these small-minded jerks. If he wanted to, he could tear the cottage down, and put up a home that would put the rest of Indian Mound look like a trailer park. But he wouldn't, because who the hell would want such crummy neighbors?

He descends into a well of anger. All he can see are cold, dark walls. He hasn't been in this space since he was a teenager, wanting to get light years away from Indian Mound. I gotta get out of this crap hole. I'm going so far away my dust will never find me. Bye-bye, Cuzzin. I'm going to be something. I'm going to be somebody. And you should, too.

And he did, and Cuzzin didn't. And now he's back, and Cuzzin's still here, and the ghosts of his parents and Uncles are all around him like the sea breeze. And don't these dumb mother fuckers realize that he has roots on Indian Mound that are deeper than their FEMA-subsidized foundations?

After several minutes, Artie realizes that he is no longer listening to a single word being said at the meeting. Shea is saying something modulated and monotonous. He stands up abruptly in mid-sentence and leaves. A few seconds later Cuzzin follows.

Hey Ah-tee, Ah-tee. Don't pay attention to them. They're scared and nervous. They took it out on you is all. Most of these people don't own much more than their houses, their cars, and their TVs. They're all mortgaged up the ying yang, so this is scary stuff. Plus, they don't understand the history or the law, so they're at a double disadvantage. They're ordinary folks. They're just scared. Hey, let's go to the cottage and hava drink.

"Cocksuckers," says Artie. "Dumb, low-life, stupid cock-suckers."

Back at the cottage, they decompress with a beer. Once Cuzzin finally succeeds in getting Artie to laugh, he hops on his Harley and leaves. Artie sits enveloped by the summer night. There's a knock, and a voice calling his name. It's Shea. Come in, he tells her, but he doesn't get up. He doesn't offer her anything.

"I want you to know that I think you were treated badly tonight."

"Thank you," he says, "but I really don't care what those people think of me."

"I know." She sits down. The room is lit to a dimness that suits Artie's brood. "With them, it's all about the buildings, the square footage, the possessions, and what you can sell them for. They just can't understand why someone like you seems to care so much about so little." She gestures around to the enveloping cottage.

"And you don't feel the same way?"

"Well, yes I do, or I did, but I've started to see the other side."

"And what's that?"

"That this place is less about shelter and possessions than about summertime, family, and community. Material things get in the way. This house is your life."

"My life is a broken down cottage?"

"That's right, but a charming, broken down cottage with a lot of character. That's why you are clinging to it so desperately."

"That's me, a truly desperate man."

"I'm sorry. It's coming out wrong. I just want you to know that those other people don't understand where you're coming from, and they treated you rudely."

"Did I miss anything of note?"

"More threats of violence. More ugly talk. More hatred. I get to try to put a positive spin on it tomorrow."

"Lucky you."

My name's Joe

Low tide is at 7 a.m. Artie is there at 6. He fishes a little, but mostly he watches. Twenty minutes after the tide change, he notices the same tailing activity.

"Now, don't spook 'em" Sandy Beach whispers in his ear. "Pay attention to the wind direction. You'll have an easier time reaching them if you are casting with the wind." Sandy has been talking to him more and more. "Instead of going directly at them, take a position down-current and move a step farther our and closer with each cast."

Artie inches towards the fish a step at a time. It takes him about five minutes to move fifty feet. His fly finally reaches the area of the tailing. Midway into his retrieve he sees the flash and swirl. He feels the tug,

He has a fish on the end of his line. He is so excited that he lets out a whoop, and Arthur Gordon hasn't whooped in so many years that his whoop is closer to a croak. There is no mistaking the exuberance.

This time the knot holds true on the fly. "Let him run," says Sandy. "Put some pressure on your reel with your hand. Don't try to tighten the drag now. Let him tire out and then lead him into shallow water."

Artie does as he is told. The fish runs out fifty feet of line, arcing his rod in a steady throb. When the fish slows, Artie reels in so that there is never any slack line. The fish's runs become short and less frequent, allowing Artie to gain ground. Now he can see the fish. It's a striper with the dignity of a judge, the power of a race car, and the sheer mass of a dirigible. The fish finally rolls to the side, and Artie is able to guide it within reach. He doesn't quite know what to do with his rod and reel (and Beach, for once, isn't there with advice), and lets it fall awkwardly in the water. He kneels in the shallow water to examine his fish.

Artie holds the fish as tenderly as he would a newborn infant. He unhooks his fly from the corner of the fish's mouth, and gently moves the fish back and forth so that water will move through its gills. The fish is much too small to be legal. Artie guesses twenty inches. When he feel the tail twitch, he knows it is time for the fish to return to the wild. He releases it and the fish hesitates for only heartbeat before swimming back to deep water.

When he picks up his rod and returns to his feet, he is startled by the sound of a single person clapping behind him and calling "Bravo!"

Joe Liquordup.

There's no facepaint or headset or headress, but the long hair and flat features are unmistakable. Jeez, he looks about Liam's age. Joe is shirtless, with his long pants rolled up to his knees, his shoulder-length hair hanging free.

"I didn't realize I was putting on a show."

"Best show in town. Is it that easy to catch a fish?"

"Easy? I've been doing this for more than a month. That's my first fish."

"What kind was it?"

"A striped bass."

"Why didn't you keep it?"

"Too small. They have to be thirty inches to be legal."

"Are they good eating?"

"The best."

"I'da kept it. And if they caught me I'd tell them that I'm a Native American, and I don't recognize the white man's fishing regulations."

There was a pause, Joe waiting to see if Artie rises to the bait.

"I can read your mind," says Joe.

"And I can read yours," says Artie.

"My job is testing the limits and pushing the buttons."

"And mine is catching fish."

"Will you teach me?"

I was just trying to get a moment of peace and quiet by coming out here I almost turned my cell phone off!. Then I hear this madman shouting at the ocean. As I came closer I saw the epic man versus fish battle. But what impressed me the most was that you were completely absorbed in what you were doing. You didn't notice me; you were completely unaware of anything but that fish on the end of your line. I recognize you from Indian Mound, so you know who I am and what I'm all about. What you don't know is that at any given moment there are a zillion things colliding in my head. There are advisors whispering in my ears, and microphones in my face, and angry people who want to sic their dogs on me. I've taken on this role willingly, but there are just times when I want it to be silent, me against the fish. Nothing else. That's what I saw on your face a few minutes ago. A little of that will go a long way for me.

But really, why should you? I'm one of those rabble-rousers who has suddenly complicated your life in ways that you didn't ask for. So, I've answered my own question. Forget I asked.

"That's all right," says Artie. "The mudflats are neutral turf, so to speak. I'm glad to pass along the little I know."

"That would be mighty white of you. My name's Joe."

Artie walks over and the men shake hands. "I know. I'm Arthur Gordon. I'm glad you saw this, because this is my first striper and I might need you to testify."

"May I see your fishing pole?" Aftie nods and hands him the fly rod. Joe starts whipping it about precariously.

"Whoa, look out! There's a very sharp hook attached to that. It wouldn't feel very good lodged in your forehead."

"Show me!" Joe continues moving the rod back and forth, trying to sense the rhythm.

I was born Henry Milliard. I didn't even know I was part Wampanoag Indian until about ten years ago when someone told my mother that fancy prep schools were offering free tuition to Native Americans. Instantly, having Indian blood went from being a curse to being a very big advantage. Even though my folks were poor, I went to all the best schools thanks to the trendiness of " diversification". I went all the way through Milton Academy, Harvard, and now Harvard Business School and never paid a cent.

"You went to Milton? So did I! Harvard, too!"

I took the name Joe Liquordup to prey on the guilt that most white Americans feel towards Native Americans. Some people feel that is biting the hand that has fed me, and I couldn't agree more, but knowing what I know, and having the skills that I have, and not using them to right some of the wrongs done to Native Americans over the centuries would be even more unconscionable.

It's irrelevant whether or not I am 100% Wompanoag or 1%. The point is that this group of people has be treated unfairly for man, many years. Anyone who does anything to improve their lot in life is doing good work. If some privileged white kid from Wellesley dedicated his life to helping the underprivileged. Everyone would regard him as a saint. I just bring a little.......theater to the situation. The press loves it, and that moves our cause along faster.

I don't get bothered by the hypocrisy of having a graduate degree from Harvard and painting my face and wearing a headdress to look like a noble savage. I can't afford to let myself think like that. I'm doing a job. I'm doing it well. No one could do it quite as well as me.

Joe is now moving the rod back and forth with more grace.

"That's it," encourages Artie, suddenly the mentor. "Let the rod throw the line. Don't feel as if you have to muscle it out."

"Cool," says Joe. Suddenly, he puts the rod in his left hand and thrusts his right into his pocket, brings out a gently vibrating cell phone. He says "yuh" four times, then folds the phone. "Looks like the lesson is over. That was fun." He hands the rod back to Artie.

"If you want to do it a little more, we've got a series of nice tides and a full moon coming up. I plan to spend about four hours a day out here. If you see me out here, come on by."

"Great. By the way, when you see me on Indian Mound I will be wearing my game face."

"Understood," says Artie.

"And," Joe hesitated, "If you can do anything to encourage your neighbors to be patient, you'll be doing them a favor."

A Scary Plan

After the fifth entreaty, Artie agrees to go up to Cuzzin's Bait & Tackle to hear the restaurant plan. It bubbles and splatters from his mouth the way clams do when lowered into the grease.

"We gotta reverse everything. Bull oriented this place to the road, but we gotta make the focus the ocean. Follow me.

"First of all, the parking lot. It's going to be crushed shells. No paving, no dust. And I'm going to get one of thos grease cars that runs on used vegetable oil. You like that. Get it all painted up, and everywhere I go, there I'll be, y'know?"

Cuzzin, a fresh beer in each hand, leads Artie across the parking lot. He has hacked an opening through the sumac and tall grasses that block off the view of the salt marsh. He has a picnic table set up. He takes a seat and opens the beers.

"See how peaceful it is here?" And it was true. The road noise was greatly diminished, making Artie aware of the noise of distant gulls. The expanse of green marsh was soothing to the eye. He was facing due west, into a restful sunset. Had Cuzzin choreographed this?

"So the plan is to get people out here as soon as possible. People will enter through the front door and come immediately to the ordah counter. They'll only be room for four, maybe five, customahs, but that's ok, because if a line spills out onto the street, people will know that we're populah.

"We take theyah drink ordah, and get 'em out here as soon as possible. Maybe give some oystah crackahs to nibble on. Thirty seconds before the food comes out, we'll announce their food, using people's first names and telling what they ordahed. None of this 'Numbah 65, your ordahs ready.' It will be 'Ah-tee, your fried clams are done, or await you.' You know, give it a little variety, a little theater. I'll do a lotta the microphone work myself. You ever heard my rich baritone over a microphone? I give good mic!

"Serve everything on paper. Keep it simple, self-bussing,

hardly any staff, 'cept in the kitchen. We'll serve the freshest seafood, perfectly cooked, and no bullshit."

Cuzzin shut up and let the sunset work for him.

"It's scary," says Artie, "but I think you've got a plan."

Liam's cell phone rings. He looks, but doesn't recognize the number.

Hello? Who? Meiko! Hey, what's up? Are you in LA? I hear you got locked out of my Father's house. So you're not mad? Cool I didn't realize you had your own place..

What's up with me? Well-l-l, there was this little incident at work. Some guys insulted my masculinity so I had to beat them up. No, not really, but let's just say my donut making career has ended. So I've been putting in time helping my Dad on the cottage.

Hey, watch your mouth! That 'nasty little cottage' is going to be mine, all mine someday.

So I'm good for that for a couple of weeks. Then school starts the last week of August. Did you hear about the Indians taking over Indian Mound? You might see it on the nightly news. It's all over the place here. Long story. Very long story.

Hm-m-m. It's possible. I'd have to run it by my Dad. As they say in Italian-"muh-funz-alo," so I'd have to ask him to stake me to airfare. He might be weird about me going out to see you. Let me pick the right time. I'll get back to you.

A Keeper

The Battle of Indian Mound continues for two weeks. July does a warm, wet smolder, interrupted by ill-tempered afternoon thunderstorms that roll in from the Berkshires. The fish can't seem to figure out what is going on. Artie tries a variety of new places between Dorchester and Hingham, but can't find any fish.

Joe Liquordup is interviewed daily, then every other day,

and now once in a while. Shea presents the public with a clear, calm front that reeks sympathy for the Native American plight while maintaining the unwavering position of the Indian Mound residents that they hold clear title to their lands, and that the activists are trespassing.

The nightly meetings produce little new information but ample amounts of bile. Artie doesn't attend, but is kept up-to-date in backyard conversations with Shea. He also gives Shea his personal opinion that when the last news crew has gone, the Wampanoags will be close behind.

"Do yourself a favor," she says, "Don't come to one of the nightly meetings with that piece of information. Patience is not a virtue with this crowd. They only respond to swear words and violence."

Artie encounters Joe several times on the mudflats, and continues to pass along his newly acquired fishing knowledge. They enjoy each other's company.

"I can't believe we went to the same prep school."

"Did you play football?"

"You mean was I a 'Mustang?' You betcha. I was the slowest and smallest second string guard in Milton Academy history."

"The school newspaper referred to me as the 'Wampanoag Wingback.'"

"Were you any good?"

"Not really. I started in my senior year, but I only caught three or four passes."

"Do you remember the school slogan?"

"Of course, 'Dare To Be True.'"

"What the hell does it mean?"

"Damned if I know."

"Pay attention to your retrieve. You're picking it up too early. Fish each cast all the way in. Remember on the last twenty feet or so to lead it off to the side, so that if a fish is following it, he won't be spooked by seeing you."

"Artie?"

"Joe?"

"Am I ever going to catch a fish, Artie?"

"Joe, you've got to believe that every single cast is going to bring a fish, because if you don't believe, how will the fish?"

"You are so full of shit."

Artie and Joe arrange to meet at 5 am. They walked to a place near Nut Island where a small salt water pond is connected to the Bay by each incoming tide.

"Look!" Artie takes Joe by the elbow and motions to the pond where ten or twelve birds are working the surface. "This is perfect. The bass have been trapped in the pond, and now the incoming tide is bringing in a fresh supply of baitfish. The bass are working them to the surface, and the birds are getting them there. Let's go in to the water over here, then work our way up slowly to the birds."

"What should we use as a fly?"

"Anything that looks like a small fish will work. Today's your day to catch a fish."

The student has become the teacher. Joe and Artie enter the water. Artie is in waders, but Joe is "wet wading" in shorts and sneakers. Joe casts with more confidence now. After each retrieve, he moves one step closer to the working birds. Artie moves with him, standing just to the left, accompanying him with a steady murmur of tips and encouragement.

The rod bends. Man and fish are joined. Joe whoops. The chase is on. The chaos is on.

The fish runs Joe's line down to the last few feet of backing. Luckily they are in a relatively open space of water and do not have to worry about the line being wrapped around rocks or pilings. Joe gains. The fish runs. Joe whoops. Artie coaches.

After a fight of nearly twenty minutes, Joe is able to work the fish to Artie, who clasps it by the lower jaw.

"This is a big fish," says Artie.

"How big do you think?"

"Let me see the fly rod. I've marked thirty inches from the butt." Joe hands him the rod. "This is at least thirty-three or four inches. You've got yourself a keeper, that is, if you want to keep it." Artie removes the hook and starts moving the fish back and forth gently.

"What are you doing?" asks Joe.

"Running some water through his gills so he can get some oxygen."

"Why are you doing that?"

"So he won't die." Joe shakes his head.

"Don't bother, because I'm keeping him."

Walking back to Indian Mound, the fish is heavy enough and awkward enough that the men have to switch off on carrying it.

"I feel like I've done a full day's work," says Joe.

"In terms of meaningful accomplishment, you have."

They were now close enough to the Mound that people on the sea wall can see they have a big fish. Joe stops and takes the fish from Artie. He holds it up high and waves triumphantly with his other hand.

"You know, time has come today."

"Time for what?"

"Time to end this silliness about the occupation of Indian Mound. Do you think you can get your people together for a meeting at noon? If we can reach a meeting of the minds, then we can hold a press conference at two and start celebrating by four or five. I can set it all in motion now."

"I'll talk to Shea. I'm sure she can meet by noon."

"Ok, we're on. One more thing, Artie. Do you know anyone who can do a clambake, the real old fashioned kind where you bury things in the sand and all that?"

"I know just the guy."

At noon Artie, Shea, and a half dozen Indian Mounders meet with Joe and his warriors by the waterfront. Joe is back in his Harvard Business School mode:

Here's the deal. We will vacate these premises tomorrow and renounce any claim on this land. In return we have only one demand and that is that Indian Mound return to its original Wampanoag name, Pissiwagasset. It means "You dig for clams over there, and I'll dig for them here." Of course what you call the community amongst yourselves is your business. You can call it "Shithole- by -the-Sea" if you want to, but on state maps and records it will be Pissiwagassett.

That's all. If we can shake on it, we'll have a brief news conference at two. The local TV stations have already been alerted. We'll have a bury-the-hatchet (ha-ha) celebration this evening, and you'll never have to see our swarthy red asses again. My guess is when you think back on this, you'll forget the hard feelings, and it will become a funny and interesting episode in the community's history.

It takes the coalition of Indian Mound, whoops Pissiwagassett residents less than a minute to reach concensus. Cuzzin is already at work down on the beach, digging a pit:

Cuzzin's Clam Bake

Dig a pit, two feet wide, eight feet long and two feet deep. Build a big motherfucking fire in it, preferably using driftwood. As the fire is burning down, line the fire pit with beach rocks. The best kind are round smooth ones, but beggars can't be choosers. Use what you got.

As the fire dies to coals, rake them to the side. Cover the rocks with a thick layer of wet rockweed seaweed. Rockweed is best because it contains tiny sacs of salt water that burst during the cooking, releasing more moisture for the steam. You will need a lot, a pick-up load or two

55 gallon drums. Layer your food in reverse order of eating. Put lobsters at the bottom, followed by shellfish, Joe's 21 pound striped bass (stuffed with onions, mint, garlic, and whatever else you want), corn, potatos, onions, eggs, and spicy sausage. My personal favorite is linguica.

Add a little more seaweed, cover with a heavy canvas tarp, and cover with sand. Let it cook for two hours. When you get ready to remove the tarp, make sure that all the other meal logistics have been taken care of-paper plates, melted butter, utensils, trash bags, ice, keg tapped-because you don't want to be interrupted once the eating begins.

The High Tide

Generally speaking the high tide belongs to the bait fisherman and the low tide to the wader. As with any good rule, this is one made to be broken. eel grass and weed beds make great hiding places for baitfish, shrimp, sand eels, and all other kinds of food. As the tide turns to outgoing, and the water begins to drain, stripers will often lie in wait so that it can drain right into their guts. The fish will hang in the deeper water and make sniper attacks as their prey moves to seaward, sometimes coming to within inches of the shoreline.

Remember that you have to expect a fish on every cast. You must believe. And you must fish each cast to the very end, as stripers are most likely to strike when they think the prey is escaping.

-- from *Think Like A Fish* by Sandy Beach

Part Three
You Can't Have it Both Ways

Chapter 8 - Bluebirds!

Sandy Beach's Fishing Forecast for August

There are lots of big fish around, but they haven't been easy to catch. In the early phases of the moon the currents are weak and wandering. This seems to make the fish lazy, and they don't feed as actively even when there are plenty of baitfish around. I'm seeing sand eels, silversides, and even small mackerel in abundance, but I've only seen the bass busting them on the surface for very short periods early in the morning and just before sunset.

I've also noticed large clouds of isopods around. This can be bad new for the striper stalker, because isopods are tiny shrimp-like organisms that stripers love. They feed on them by getting right in the cloud, usually just below the surface, opening their mouths, closing their eyes and lollygaging about, practically inhaling their food. When fish are this fat, dumb, and happy, even the best-presented fly will not be effective. About the only thing you can do is cast the loudest surface-popping fly and try to taunt the fish into striking. It's the fly fishing equivalent to insulting their masculinity, but it can shake them from their stupor.

The good news is that the isopods can disappear instantly, and it doesn't take the bass long to remember their predatory instincts, so don't stop fishing. My bones tell me to expect good things, especially as we march toward the full moon.

    -Sandy Beach, from *The Boston Globe*

In that case

Artie awakes with Shea nestled onto his right shoulder. He remembers the sequence of events. There was the clambake. Indian Mound was officially renamed as Pissawaggassett. Cuzzin officially announced that he was going into the restaurant business. Kegs were tapped, beer was drunk.

More beer was drunk.

A bonfire was started. Someone said that all that was missing was music. Cuzzin got the bright idea to take four guys and his truck to the cottage to get Artie's piano. Within minutes Artie was performing from the bed of Cuzzin's truck, leading the residents of Indian Mound and a now congenial band of Wampanoags in singing the three chord chestnuts from the 50s and 60s.

More beer was drunk.

Artie remembers playing "Diana," "Maybe," "Great Balls of Fire," "Good Golly Miss Molly," "Tutti Frutti," "Long Tall Sally," "Teenager in Love." He remembers singing "March, March On Mustangs," the Milton Academy fight song with Joe. He can remember his entire play list, but he can't quite remember how Shea came to be in his bed.

Did they make love? Artie has vague recollections of fondling and kissing. Ah, now he remembers:

Shea had too much to drink, or so she said.

After about a ten minute rendition of his signature "Whole Lotta Shakin'" a gaggle of about ten semi-plastered Injuns and Pissawagassians (as they dubbed themselves) led, of course, by the ubiquitous, rabble-rousing Cuzzin, managed to wrestle the piano back into the cottage. Then the noisy contingent pinballed their way back to the keg, and somehow Shea was left with Artie. She was still glowing from the sudden end of hostilities and asked Artie if he had a glass of wine. She was effusive in her praise for his musicianship and how he had been the only person to bridge the gap between the locals and the Wompanoags.

She had another glass of wine and sat next to Artie, much too close, on the couch. At the end of the second glass she announced "I've had too much to drink. I've got to go to bed."

Artie said he'd walk her home, but she said "I'll never make it that far. I can only make it as far as your bed." She wasn't slurring her words.

Artie took her in, got her comfortably situated. She was wearing shorts and a cotton jersey, so he didn't bother undressing her, just plopped her down, covered, and sat on the bed and tucked her in. When she seemed to be happily drifting off, he got up to leave.

"Where are you going?" she said, suddenly alert.

"To sleep on the couch."

"Oh no you don't." She reached out and pulled his arm. "You're sleeping with me. You don't have to do anything more than hold me, but you're staying with me."

Elaine Gives Good Phone

Artie quietly got up to pee and to check his cell phone messages. There was one from Elaine that came around 6 pm, asking him to call right back. Then there was one from her at

7 pm, 8 pm, and finally one at 9 pm that said she was on her way to LAX Airport to catch a red-eye to Boston. Her voice sounded agitated, but not dire. His best guess was that the Meiko thing had somehow exploded and that she was up to some vindictive mischief.

What the hell is going on? He tried to think through the possibilities. What would require Elaine's physical presence? And why didn't she just leave an explanation. He walked back to the bedroom. Oh yeah. Shea. For a moment he had forgotten.

What the hell is going on?

She's now stirring. She opens her eyes. "This could go either way," Artie says to himself. She smiles. Whew.

"Talk to any possums lately?" she asks.

"Not last night. Surprised?" he asks.

"About talking to possums?"

"About being here?"

"Oh no," she says calmly. Somehow during the night her clothes had been removed. "I've planned this for a long time."

"You're kidding! How long a time?"

"Maybe a week. I didn't know exactly how, where, or when, but I knew. And you know what?" She pulls Artie down into the bed with her.

"What?" He knows he's being toyed with, but he doesn't mind.

"The next time you get to fuck me."

"Hm-m-m-m. Well, that may not be tonight, because I just heard from my agent that she's taking the red-eye from LA to tell me something, but I don't have any idea what's up."

"In that case," says Shea, "You get to fuck me now."

"I take mine black." Shea is in the primitive kitchen of the cottage, wearing her clothes from yesterday.

"I'm surprised you let a vile drug like caffeine pass into that temple of a body" says Artie, pouring her a mug.

"I haven't had coffee since last March. I've been healing."

"Healing from what?"

"Long story, another time."

"So what changed your opinion about me?"

"Little things. When you first came, I was a too sensitive and over-reacted to you. I took your ineptness personally, but I came to realize that you are not malicious so much as clueless. I've been able to see how you are with your son and cousin. You're a decent guy. And with this deal with the Indians, you were the only voice of sanity. Also, I rented the video of *My Mother, My Lover, My Wife, and Now, My Sales Manager*, and I can see you're a pretty accomplished director."

"Like it?"

"I did. Very much. It made me realize that we're in the same boat licking our wounds. We're both on the mend. It made me think we could help each other out."

The cab pulls up and Elaine wobbles out. She is disoriented. Luckily, Artie is there to greet her.

Elaine is short, with dark, curly hair now migrating to gray. She has been slim all her life, but now is fighting the battle of middle age bulge. She's dressed entirely in black, with footwear that makes no sense whatsoever on Indian Mound. The cabby pulls her bag from the trunk. She hands him a bill that generates an enthusiastic thank-you.

"Hey, Beautiful."

"Artie. Look at you!." Artie is dressed in what has become his daily costume-a clean, but wrinkled t-shirt, blue shorts, and that's it. For formal occasions he wears sandals. Other than that, the only clothes he wears are waders. "So tanned! Aside from the fact that you look like a bum, you look great."

"Elaine, it's great to see you, but what the hell's going on?"

"First, coffee."

"I've got some made."

Artie, this coffee isn't half-bad, but the most remarkable feature is that I notice two dirty cups You got a companion you haven't told me about? Artie? Ar-tie? Whatever! You're a big boy.

Everything is fine, but life takes some interesting turns. My Mother, My Lover is still number one both in video sales and rentals. And this is with no media at all, unless you want to count your disastrous public relations. I think what's going on is that the nerve we thought this movie would touch was there all along. People just couldn't explore it in public by going to the theater, so they had to wait until they could see it in the privacy of their homes.

Yes, just like pornography.

By the way, I can't believe you are living in this shack. It's like camping out, but more primitive.

You think I'm staying here? What are you, nuts?

So your contract with the studio gave them a ninety-day option on the rights for any kind of sequel based on the original. The standard boilerplate. My Mother, My Lover was released on March 15 (beware the Ides of fucking, March, right Artie?) so the option expired on June 15.

June 15 comes and goes. I didn't even call them to see if they were interested because on June 15 you ranked right up there with Hitler and the Boston Strangler on the popularity charts. Then on July 1 the movie is released on video, and by July 12, without any studio support, it's #1.

Now it's been #1 for three straight weeks, and even more interestingly, it's getting stronger each week. No one's ever seen a sales and rental pattern like this. So two days ago I get a call from that schmuck Lipshitz at the studio. Imagine having that little pissant call about anything. He makes nice and then slides in the fact that I must have made an oversight by not calling them on the option, but he'll be a nice guy and not let my incompetence get in the way of a business deal.

One side of me is glad we're getting the option picked up, because a hundred grand is a hundred grand, but another side of me is really pissed that they'd be calling with someone so low on the food chain. It's an insult to me, and a slap in the face to you. Lipshitz, for chrissakes.

I'm listening to him run on about how great they are to be exercising the option, because, you know, who woulda thought they'd consider making a sequel to the world's biggest turkey when Stephanie bursts into the office and hands me a slip of paper that says one word, "Spielberg!!"

"I gotta go," I tell the little prick. Then I switch lines:

"Stephen! How are you?" Like I've ever met the guy. Actually I have, but I didn't think he'd ever remember. But he does. Then he starts making small talk. SMALL TALK! Stephen Spielberg is asking me what I think is going on in the business these days. Then he tells me the reason for the call is to see if Jasper Mumphrey is making progress on his novel. Jasper Mumphrey, Jesus! I mean, I represent the guy, and I even kind of like him, but everyone in town knows that until he goes through re-hab you might as well be asking about Buster the Wonder Dog.

I tell him that Jasper's been under the weather. And he says to let him know if anything develops, and then he sneaks in, "Oh, what's Arthur Gordon up to these days?"

Jackpot.

Now I know he's in the hunt for My Mother, My Lover, *but I'm cool. Artie you'da been very proud of me. I say "He's spending a lotta time fishing." You like that? "A lotta time fishing."*

And he says "I like fishing. Maybe Arthur and I can go together sometime. Did Sony pick up the option of My Mother, My Lover? I tell him "no," and he says, "Well, Dream Works is interested. You talk to Arthur much?" Of course, I lie and tell him I'm seeing you tomorrow. He says "Ask him what his plans are. Maybe we can work together."

"Yeah," I say, "I'll try to remember."

Then he says, you'll love this, "Promise me you won't commit to anyone on this until you've talked to me."

Do you believe that? Stephen Spielberg saying to me P r o m i s e …me … you …won't …commit …to …anyone until …you've …talked …to …me.

Artie tells Elaine she should take a nap, but she is so caught up in the chase, that she can't consider sleep. She wants to put the film rights to My Mother, My Lover up for auction while the interest is hot. She's come to Boston anticipating some hot and heavy negotiating that will need Artie's immediate input. Artie, however, has other plans.

"Low tide is at 1:36 pm. I want to explore Germantown Flats when I can see the structure and learn about the current and flow of the tides. You can come along."

"Like this?"

"I'll outfit you."

"By the way, I heard back from the research department on your friend, Sandy Beach."

"Really!" Artie is suddenly leaning forward. "What did you learn?"

"There is no Sandy Beach, at least not any more. There was a guy by that name who wrote a fishing column for The Boston Globe back in the late 1950s. His biggest claim to fame was that he was a fishing buddy of Ted Williams. But he died while fishing in Tortola in 1960."

"Natural causes?"

"Suspicious circumstances. He was found floating face down in about eighteen inches of water, wearing all his fishing gear. Apparently, Beach wasn't entirely reliable as a Globe columnist, so a lot of his work was ghosted by other staffers. When they heard he died, they already had been cobbling together the column for a while, so they just kept doing it. Over the years they've produced books, columns, and all kinds of other material under the name of Sandy Beach."

"Something is fishy here. Wouldn't his family object?"

"But here's the rub, 'Sandy Beach' wasn't his own name. He was already using a pseudonym."

"Interesting. Hm-m-m. That explains some things, but also raises some new questions."

"You haven't asked his real name."

"I'll bite. What was his real name?"

"Gordon Arthur."

Artie still wears his tee shirt and shorts, but he now has a long-billed cap and polarized sunglasses. Elaine is similarly attired in Artie's clothes. Her cell phone is glued to her ear. They are walking on the exposed mudflats of Germantown, surrounded by eelgrass. Her legs are like porcelain piano legs.

Stephanie, it's me. I'm here with Artie. It wasn't so bad. I took a sleeping pill. You wouldn't believe where we are. I'm in the middle of a mudflat, with mud squishing between my toes. Artie's checking out the place for fishing. I feel like I'm on a different planet. Any calls?

Oh-h-h! OH-H-H-H! So Mr. Big Cheese finally is calling. I guess Mr. Lipschitz got the message that this wasn't going to be a gimmee. When did he call? Twice? I'll call him back. Don't leave the phone. There's going to be lots of activity this morning.

Artie is making notes in his log. It's about fifteen minutes from low tide. The area is well protected from wind. A clam bed has been exposed, along with a few rocks with mussels clinging to them. A smooth slick extends out into the bay, indicating where the outgoing tide is meeting deeper water. This could be a comfortable place for bass to rest. Then, as the tide turns, they come in over the clam and mussel beds looking for what has been left behind.

Artie takes the temperature of the water. 71 degrees. He nods when Elaine says, much too loud, "I knew it! Sidney Miller's called! Twice! That little prick Lipschitz must have felt this one slipping away. Let's see what Mr. Studio President has to say for himself."

Sidney! Elaine Siegal. How are you, Sweetie? I'm perfect, maybe better. No I'm out of town. In fact I'm visiting Arthur Gordon at his seaside villa on Cape Cod? Just a little R & R.

Really? That is a coincidence. I can't really put him on the line,

Sidney, because he's been very emphatic about no business talk. But that's him, not me. I can talk business. You know me. The store is always open. 24/7. What are you thinking about?

Uh-huh.......uh-huh.........uh-huh.......uh-huh.......uh-huh. Well, that's a little better than what Dipshit called with yesterday. I didn't think he could really be representing your views on this project, Sidney. Oh, yes, I know how you've always been supportive of this project, even when the going got a little rough. Seems like ancient history, doesn't it? Who'd of thought that we'd be laughing about Sixty Minutes one day.

I couldn't agree more! Mike Wallace is a shriveled old cocksucker who should have been sent off to the glue factory years ago.

Let me try to find Arthur to tell him about this. I think he's out fishing. I call you back, Sweetie.

"Artie, do I give good phone or do I give good phone? Miller, is offering a half-million, plus full artistic control. I'm sure he'll go three, four times that when he hears Dream Works is in the picture."

The tide has reached dead low. There's no signal, no sound. Just a momentary stillness, then an imperceptible change in motion. He sketches what it looks like at dead low.

"Don't forget, you need a visual reference." It was Sandy Beach talking to Artie. He had told him this more than once. In fact his column that morning was on this exact subject.

It's very easy for a fisherman to become so caught up in the thrill of the chase, that he forgets that the tide stops for no man. If you have waded out on the outgoing tide, and you don't follow the tide in, you can find yourself swimming, and that's not easy with a nine-foot fly rod.

The way around this is to establish a fixed visual reference at low tide that you can glance at and instantly get a sense of the tide's progression. This simple tip has kept me from being stranded many times, but it took a few dunkings to teach me.

"What can I tell him, Artie? Want me call Spielberg? Maybe we should involve Universal. Not that we'd do anything with them, but they might drive up the bid. This is beautiful. We've got about six options here. Whaddya think?"

Artie looks directly at her:

I think I better be careful wading here. I need a visual reference. The way the tide comes in over that bar, and the holes that exist between here and the shore mean you could get cut off if you aren't careful. There's plenty of food here. Find the food; find the fish. It might be fun to try a crab imitation here, because, as the tide turns, the bass will scoot in looking for anything that has been in its terrestrial mode. I think this place is definitely worth a shot.

"Oh." She is puzzled. "You're talking about fish. Real fish. I'm talking about big fish."

"Elaine, do you ever hear voices, like someone speaking right in your ear?"

"Yes, Artie. About two minutes ago Stephen Fucking Spielberg was speaking right in my ear, and he was saying that he will pay many dollars for the rights to make the sequel to *My Mother, My Lover*. So now will you now get with the program and get some of your greed juices flowing. Don't you appreciate how the worm has turned?"

"Where did that phrase come from?"

"From the ancient Chinese. How the fuck do I know, Artie? What are we going to tell these guys now that we've got their attention."

Artie continues his inspection of Germantown Flats, overturning rocks and inspecting their undersides.

"I hear what you are saying, Elaine, and you're beautiful, and I love you, and the world's best agent, not to mention best friend, and you're not going to like this, but I want to take things slow. It's not the best negotiating ploy, and it may not net the biggest bucks. I want to figure out what's best for me, and right now, I really don't know."

Elaine suddenly sputters squeals of fright and disgust. "There are little things bumping into my feet!"

"Those are shrimp, just like you eat, but tiny."

"I don't like them. Ouch! I stepped on a piece of glass!"

"Probably a clamshell. Are you bleeding?"

Elaine grabs her foot and looks at her sole. "I don't think so. Jesus, Artie, what do you want me to do? Let me put it in your terms. We've big fish fighting to bite our bait. When they do, we need to reel them in!"

"What are my options?"

" OK, here they are. #1 Do nothing. Just sit with your thumb up your ass, live in your shack, bypass millions of dollars, and let your reputation remain in the shitter."

Artie pulls apart a clamshell and finds it filled with mud. "OK, I understand #1."

"#2, sell the rights, let Spielberg or Sony make the sequel. You get a pile of money. You get no say in the production at all. It's their baby. #3, put it up for auction, tell everyone it's for sale with you as director, don't ask for any points and hope they start a bidding war. And #4, work out a friendly deal, with you getting a lower fee upfront, a percentage of the gross, and full artistic control."

"Any other options?"

"One more. Keep the rights. Take the independent route. Make the film yourself. Do a distribution deal with one of the studios, and live or die with the outcome."

Artie drops the rock onto the mud. He extends his arm and draws Elaine to him.

"You are the best agent in the world. That's why I've been with you for more than twenty years; that's why you're my son's Godmother; that's why I love you."

Elaine leans her head into his chest for a second, then says

"Cut the crap, Artie. What do you want to do?"

"You must be incredibly tired after the red-eye."

"Cut the crap, Artie. What do you want to do?"

"I want to gather my loved ones around me and have them help me with this decision."

"Cut the crap, Artie. What do you want to do?"

"That's really what I want to do. I'm going to take you back to the cottage and put you down for a nap. I'm going to call Liam, Cuzzin, and my next door neighbor, and invite them to dinner tonight."

"What do I tell Sidney and Spielberg?"

"Don't tell them a thing. Take the phone off the fucking hook, or whatever the cell phone equivalent is."

Liam! Are you free tonight? Elaine's in town and I'd like to have a special dinner for her at Anna's. She'd love to see you. Great! By the way, I'm going to ask Shea to join us .Is that a problem for you? Well, we're getting along better. Sure, I can meet you a few minutes early. What's the subject? Not even a hint? OK, I can wait. Dinner's at seven. Can you come down at six? See you then.

Hey, Cuzzin. Are you available for dinner tonight? Anna's at seven? Last night was fun. More than you'll ever know. Oh, you already know. I should have known. I've got a surprise. You do, too? Cool! Anna's at seven.

Shea, Artie. Howyadoin'. Hey, my agent, Elaine, is in town, and I'm taking her dinner at Anna's tonight with Liam and Cuzzin. It's kind of a celebration. Will you join us? Great! Seven. You can ride with us.

Tell me the Truth

Artie puts on a polo shirt, his dress shorts, and sandals. He shaves, and after a moment of contemplation, puts on a drop of after-shave. He's clean, slightly sun and windburned from the Flats, and feeling good about the world. He is making himself a gin and tonic when Liam comes in.

"Hey, Sonny. Would you like a g & t?"

"What's that?"

"A gin & tonic."

"Gin, bleuch-h-h."

"Sometimes you have to accept that not everything in life tastes sweet. Here, take mine, I'll make another." Liam takes a sip.

"Crackly," he says.

"The bubbles wake up your throat, the gin comes slicing through, and then the lime explodes into your nostrils." He stirs his drink with his finger, and holds out a glass to toast, "Here's to whatever you want to talk to me about."

Liam clinks his glass. "I'm not so sure how you'll feel about this in about thirty seconds."

I've had a few phone calls recently from Meiko. We had fun going to the clubs when she was out here. No big deal. Mostly swapping notes on different bands and stuff. Anyway, she's asked me to come out and spend a couple of weeks hanging out with her before school starts. I'd kind of like to do it. I haven't been back to California for a while. But I don't have the money, so I'd have to ask you, but I know this might be a sensitive subject for you so I thought we could talk it over.

"Did you have sex with her while she was out here?"

"No, I swear to God!"

"Tell me the truth, Liam!"

"I'm telling you the truth!"

"TELL ME THE TRUTH!"

Liam, quietly, "I'm telling you the truth."

"Ok, I believe you. Jesus Christ. I don't believe this. You know what's happening, don't you, Liam?"

"What?"

"She's using you to get back at me. I don't know what her game is. Leading you along and breaking your heart. Giving you a venereal disease. Telling you what an asshole I am. I'm not sure what she's doing, but I guarantee you're a pawn in her game."

"I'd be crazy not to recognize that you might be right, but I don't think you are. I think we just hit it off, so she's saying 'come out to LA,' and I'd like to do it. I'll keep my eyes open. I'm a big boy now."

"You're 21!" says Artie. "You're still a boy to me. I can't help it. And that's another thing. She's 24. Why does a 24-year-old want to hang out with a 21-year-old. C'mon. How sick is that?"

Liam is smart enough to let the silence speak.

"Ok," says Artie. "I take your point. Did you call your mother on this? And what did she say"

"To follow my bliss."

"Oh my fucking word! Listen, Liam….I'm not trying to be a jerk, but there's no way I see this as anything but big trouble."

"How about we seek a second opinion?" says Liam.

"Who do you have in mind?"

"Uncle Cuzzin."

Artie stares into his gin & tonic, which now has lost its fizz and appeal. He downs it in a single swallow.

Anna Scaffidee's Mint Sauce for Fish

Warm olive oil and lightly sauté LOTS of garlic. Add white wine and vinegar to taste.

Simmer for ten minutes.

Add a handful (one per frying pan) of mint leaves.

Add one cup of frush (fresh and crushed) tomatoes.

Ladle over white fish. Haddock is best.

Vroom-vroom

"I'll order for the entire table," says Artie.

Anna's is buzzing. Everyone looks very spiffy and alluring. There is one empty chair. The waitress stands poised and ready.

"We'll start with a bottle of the sparkling Moet champagne. If it's not cold enough, I'll send it back, and if you don't have at least five bottles, tell me so I can order something else. When one bottle is empty just bring another. Don't ask.

"We'll start with two orders of onion rings. Follow that with green salads all around. Then bring us three orders of steamed clams. Those are fresh, right? Where are they from? OK.

"Then bring the entree of Anna's Haddock With Mint Sauce with steamed new potatoes and whatever. Which is better, the green beans or zucchini? OK then, we'll go with the zucchini. Could you put a little parmesan and fresh ground pepper on that. Tell you what, do it at the table. Thanks.

"People can order their own desserts, although I can tell right now I want the Indian Pudding with hard sauce. And don't start bringing the food, except the champagne and onion rings, until Cuzzin gets here, which, from the sound of it, won't be too long."

Everyone agreed that Artie had done a masterful job of ordering. The only missing piece was for Cuzzin to arrive. As is often the case, he can be heard before seen.

"What's that?" asks Elaine. Someone, or something, has put the bar area into an uproar.

"Either Nomar has just put one out of the park, or our boy has arrived."

Vroom-vroom-vroom. He ripples through the room like a sandpaper wave. Pebbles falling into a pot.

Suddenly he appears.

There is silence.

There is confusion.

This is Cuzzin. Then he laughs.

This is Cuzzin!

Making Up Games

"How do you like the new me?" Cuzzin has been shaved and shorn. He is clothed in a suit and tie. He smells good. He is entirely transformed from a paunchy piece of gristle, until he opens his mouth.

"And who is this tasty morsel?" he says, looking at Elaine.

"This is Elaine, my agent. We're celebrating, a little prematurely, but celebrating nonetheless," says Artie. The waitress brings the first bottle of bubbly.

"I'm celebrating, too," says Cuzzin, then aside to the waitress, "Bring me a club soda, willya."

Liam falls off his chair.

"It's simple," says Cuzzin, pressed for an explanation. "Tomorrow I go to the bank to see if they'll loan me money for the restaurant, because someone sitting at this table can't make up his mind whether or not he wants to be my partner. I asked myself this morning 'Would I take this guy seriously?

Would I loan me a half a million bucks?' The answer was a resounding NO. If I'm going to ask the banker to dance, I better look like someone worth dancing with."

"Then, will you go back to being Cuzzin?"

"Oh, shit yeah." The whole tables vroom-vrooms.

"Tell me about this restaurant," says Elaine, not realizing that she has opened the door to the entire saga of the Gordon's critical, but largely unrecognized role in the development of the fast-food industry in America and the world. She actually seems interested.

Artie is digging into his Indian Pudding when Shea asks "What are we celebrating?"

"There's so much to celebrate," says Artie. "I don't know where to begin. Indian Mound or Pissawagassett has been returned to its owners in more ways than one. Elaine, my agent and Liam's godmother, is here. Cuzzin has decided what he wants to be when he grows up. Shea and I have overcome our differences. (Cuzzin can't resist a subliminal vroom.) Nucking Fuff construction has gotten the cottage into shape......"

"And Stephen Spielberg wants to make the sequel to My Mother, My Lover...!" blurts Elaine.

"We haven't decided which way to go with it," hastens Artie.

"But in any case," adds Elaine, "Hollywood's biggest loser is soon-to-be Hollywood's biggest winner."

"I thought maybe you had caught your fish." says Cuzzin. "Who's Stephen Spielberg?"

Over coffee, the family council goes into executive session. First Artie presents the Meiko situation, then Liam follows with his own version.

"If you don't go, I will. That girl was hot!" Cuzzin is unequivocal in his support.

"We're asking advice from the most irresponsible man on the face of the earth," says Artie.

"I'm not kidding," says Cuzzin, "Meiko was the nicest piece of ass to ever hit the South Shore. Who cares if he gets used, so long as he gets used, if know what I mean." Lubba-lubba, vroom-vroom.

"Elaine, what do you say?"

"I always liked Meiko. A spaceshot, but all your girlfriends are, Artie. She was very calm when I called her about getting her things. She said 'I know all about The Drill. You won't get any problem from me. I'm the one who broke it off anyway.' And having come here to your cottage, Artie, I've gotta say she had a decent reason to be upset."

Liam says, "What do you think, Shea?"

Shea smiles, obviously pleased at being part of the family council. "I think you have to go by the record. Liam's been very responsible all summer. He's done everything asked. He's helped around the cottage. If he wants to do this, and you've told him about the potential pitfalls, you should trust him to do the right thing."

"Ok," says Artie, putting his hands on the table, signaling acceptance, "but there's got to be a quid pro quo, something I get out of the deal."

"What do you want?" asks Liam.

"I know how seductive the scene out there can be. You've got to promise me, no matter what, you will come back and finish your last semester at Berklee."

They shake.

More on band names from Liam:

I think now that I'm going to call my band RE:AM. First of all, it just sounds good, like you know this band can really rock. If nothing else you've got four-fifths of "scream" in the name.

I like the gender neutrality of "ream." Plus, there's a suggestion of violence to it. Well, maybe more than a suggestion. Maybe a lot more.

But there are other overtones, too. There's a "ream" of paper to give it a literary association. By capitalizing it and adding the colon, you accomplish two things. First of all, you're only one letter away from R.E.M., one of my favorite old-time bands and a heavy influence on Nirvana. But by separating "ream" with the colon, the meaning becomes "in reference to being." Get it? "Re" as in "regarding" or "in reference to" and "am" as in "I am," or, more specifically, as in "I think, therefore I am."

I've never quite understood what it means, and I forget who said it, but he was a famous philosopher. "I think, therefore I am." I don't get it, but I'm sure some critic who is a lot smarter than I am will find deep, cosmic meaning, especially if our music is good.

If the music is bad, this will be seen for the shallow, superficial pretension that it is.

An Indian Mound tradition is making up games. There were a few tattered board games, jigsaw puzzles that could be put together in minutes, and a deck of cards for rainy days, but otherwise the summers of Artie's youth were spent in an almost complete void of toys. Until he learned differently as an adult, Artie thought that mumblety-peg was a game made up by Tubby Tropiano. Similarly, games like kick the can, red rover/red rover, flashlight tag, and hide & seek were all customized to their seaside location. There was never a television in the cottage.

Indian Mound was not about being entertained, but rather, about being so bored that you find ways to entertain yourself. Liam and Artie are ferociously competitive with a game they've invented which involves kicking field goals with a styrofoam coffee cup from Dunkin' Donuts. You get three points for kicking it into the trashcan, plus one additional point for each step you are away from the can. Near misses count for naught. By mid-August the cumulative score is Liam 48- Artie 44. Both men have adopted the strategy of kicking relatively easy short field goals. Longer kicks are reserved for desperation catch-up situations. First one to reach 50 wins. They're still talking about the 10 yarder that Liam nailed when Artie was ahead 32-25 and threatening to blow the game wide open. But Liam came through in the clutch to vault ahead 35-32 and hasn't looked back since.

Liam tees his cup up on the grass. He concentrates, takes a deep breath, kicks ... wide right. Artie picks up the cup and follows the same ritual. His kick is up, a perfect end-over-end, it catches the back lip of the trashcan, and bounces in!

"YES! YES! The grizzled veteran comes through, and suddenly all the pressure is on the kid. This is choke time. This is when you need nerves of steel, not butterflies in the stomach. If you make it, I get a last kick."

"No you don't. First one to fifty is what we said."

"I know, but you kicked first."

"I won the toss!"

"That doesn't mean you get an extra kick."

"What is it about 'First one to 50 wins' that you don't understand?"

"You'll probably choke, and I'll win anyway. I wouldn't even want to win if I was winning just because I had more chances that the other guy."

"OK, suppose I make mine, giving me 51 points, and then

you make yours, giving you 50. Who wins then?"

"It's a tie."

"A tie!" Liam is apoplectic. "How can you have a 51-50 tie!"

"We've both made it to 50 with the same number of kicks. We'll have to devise some kind of a tie-breaker."

"Sudden death or tennis format?"

"I dunno. I haven't thought it through."

"Let's finish this out."

"Keep kicking."

Artie fishes the cup out of the trashcan and flips it to Liam. He talks with the upper epiglottal thrust of a sportscaster: "Liam Gordon will now make what is undoubtedly the biggest kick of his young life. A hush falls over the huge throng at Indian Mound Stadium as he tees up the cup. Now he adjusts it. He stands over it, his mind racing with the implications of failure. He kicks ... it's wide right, wide right! He had the distance, but he pushed it to the right. And now, it's up to the Old Man."

Arthur lowers his voice dramatically as he picks up the cup and places it just so. "It all comes down to this, and how many times have we seen the Old Man come through in situations like this? The crowd is on its feet, but the Old Man doesn't show a flicker of emotion. He's been through it all before." Artie kicks a low line drive that hits the trashcan about a foot off the ground. Now, it's Liam's turn to be animated.

"He skulls it. What a choke! He's been there before and he's choked before!" He places the cup and deftly lofts it into the can with his foot. "And it's all over! It's all over. Arthur Gordon has snatched the agony of defeat from the jaws of victory."

"Wait a minute. I still get my last kick."

Sony makes a "pre-empt" bid for the film rights to make a sequel of *My Mother, My Lover...* of $2 million, meaning that their bid needs to be accepted or rejected before the property is offered to others. Artie, through Elaine, rejects it.

Stephen Spielberg, casually, calls to see how Artie's summer is going. Artie tells he's been trying to catch a fish. "Moby Dick?" asks Spielberg. Artie invites him to come to Indian Mound and to try his luck. Spielberg says he just might, and meanwhile, give him a call when he decides which route he wants to follow with the sequel. "I don't mind being patient, but I do mind being asleep at the switch, and that's what I'll feel like if someone else signs this up while I'm being patient," says Spielberg. Don't, he reiterates, make a commitment before checking with him.

Elaine, who has been on the cell phone nearly non-stop since her arrival, finally crashes. She sleeps for twenty straight hours. When she finally rises, Artie makes her coffee. They're sitting at the kitchen table and she says, "So, this cousin of yours, is he married?"

Artie looks at her dumbly, trying to contemplate the strands in the universe that have connected. Life just doesn't make sense. Or does it? The Red Sox, meanwhile, are in second place, behind the Yankees. They appear to have a good shot at a wild card slot in the playoffs.

Cuzzin comes by that evening. He brings a half-bushel of oysters and a fresh bluefish that someone gave him at the bait shop. He is fresh from the bank, wearing his suit and looking good. His mood, however, is low:

"They'll loan me up to the value of the real estate, which is two hundred grand, but they think my estimate for renovations is too low. And my business track record and credit history are, in the words of Mr. DeFalco at the bank, 'on the light side.' That's when I lost all respect for him. Anyone calling my business track record 'on the light side' doesn't know crap about business." He pauses. A little vroom-vroom-vroom.

"And my credit history 'on the light side?' Puh-leese. Can't we agree it's completely 'on the dark side?' Jay-sus. I didn't file my income taxes for eight years. My credit cards are long gone. I'm two months behind on my rent. I owe small change to every bar within 10 miles. My shop has not shown a profit in five years. My checking balance is -$25. C'mon, that is not 'on the light side!' That is on the heavy, fuckin' dark side."

This put him in a much better mood. VROOM-VROOM-LUBBADUBBA-VROOM. "How can you be the quintessential fuck-up and not be insulted when a pissant banker says you 'on the light side'?"

Cuzzin shows Elaine how to properly shuck and eat an oyster. She gives him her rapt attention.

Cuzzin's How-to Oyster Guide

First of all, only eat oysters from cold water. I've had those flabby oysters from the Gulf of Mexico. You might as well be eating tofu on a shell, for chrissakes.

I use a screwdriver to open oysters. An oyster knife is good, too. Everyone has their own technique, but don't use a sharp knife. You'll wreck the knife, and if you slip, you can cause yourself grievous damage. Oysters should be kept cold and eaten cold. This West Coast thing of barbecuing oysters? It's bullshit. The only reason they do it that way is because they are too damn lazy to do it the right way, so they put them on a grill. That way they don't have to deal with the oyster's firm grasp on life. Don't get me started on the West Coast. Not only do they eat the oyster hot, but they cover up the flavor with hot sauce. Passive aggressive motherfuckers! That's what happens when life is too easy.

Wear a heavy glove on your left hand if you're right-handed, on your right if you are a lefty. Helpful hint: throw the other glove away immediately. Otherwise you end up with a drawerful of right-handed gloves. Don't believe me? Check the third drawer of the porch bureau.

Put the oyster in your left hand, with the deep side of the shell down and the hinge facing toward you. This is very important. Jam the tip of screwdriver into the hinge of the oyster, and give it a good twist. If you do it right, she'll pop. If you are a little off, which is easy to do, you'll end up with a chipped shell, and the fun will just have begun. What follows is often not pretty.

Pry the shallow half of the shell off, using a knife to scrape any flesh into the deep half. Make sure not to lose any of the liquor, or juice from the deep half. Run your blade under the oyster to make sure it is free of the shell.

Rotate the oyster 180 degrees, without spilling any liquor, so that thin edge is facing you. Slide it, liquor and all, right into your mouth. Chew it two or three times, just enough to taste the sea, then let it slither down to your gullet.

You may now take a sip of beer.

I know some people arrange them on shaved ice, and serve them with lemon wedges or cocktail sauce, but those things just get in the way. You could eat a cold turd with enough cocktail sauce. Eat the oyster the way a starfish would, as close to live as possible and as close to the sea as possible.

Grilled Bluefish a la Artie

Bluefish is a very oily fish. Because of this, I'm not sure why, the flavor deteriorates very quickly. Never buy bluefish in a market, even a good fish market, and never, never order bluefish in a restaurant.

That said, fresh bluefish can be one of the most delicious things you will ever taste. I cook mine on the grill, over a bed of hardwood charcoal. Don't use compressed briquettes, and for god's sake, don't use charcoal starter.

This doesn't make sense, but coat your bluefish fillets with mayonnaise. I know it sounds disgusting, and it makes even less sense, but it works. I've asked chefs to explain this to me, and none of them can. Somehow the mayonnaise does something chemical with the oil in the flesh.

Whatever! The mayonnaise makes the bluefish delicious. Trust me.

The hardest part is flipping the filet, because if it sticks to the grill, you will end up serving a lump of baked mess. The best protection is to make sure your fire is hot, and the grill is clean. You can brush the grill with olive oil just prior to serving.

Bluefish tastes great with freshly ground pepper. The mayonnaise disappears in the cooking process. It emulsifies, or something. You can also do fancy things with bluefish and people will really think you know what you are doing. I've served bluefish on a bed of steamed onion. Once I made a little confit of chopped fresh tomato (remember to remove the seeds) and black olives.

Don't insult bluefish with white wine.

> *Bluefish can stand up to even the most challenging red. I like to match it with one of those arrogant Italian wines such as a Barolo or a Barbaresco. A bluefish fights just as ferociously in your mouth as it does in the salt water. If you can find some of those rugged red table wines from Corsica or Sardinia, even better.*

What Really Pisses Me Off

"May I come?"

Artie is rigging up for his daily striper search. He isn't prepared for Shea's question.

"I'll just bring my chair and a book. It's a beautiful day." She holds up her lawn chair. It's one of the low-slung kind, perfect for sitting just above the lapping waves.

Elaine has returned to L.A. Ain't no Injuns around. The Sox are still in the running for the wild card. Liam is getting ready to go visit Meiko. Cuzzin, Artie, and Shea are all trying to figure out what to do with their lives. August is suddenly in a holding pattern, with dank, humid air forcing the residents of the North End out onto their balconies to sleep.

"Well, ok," his reluctance shows, "but I have to warn you that I concentrate very hard when I fish. And we'll be doing some walking. The day Elaine came with me was just a scouting expedition, and she was a pain in the ass."

"I won't be. I promise and walking is ok."

August has just passed the tipping point. You can't say that there is a nip of fall in the air, because it's over 80 degrees, but something has changed. The tomatoes know it. The stripers know it. Shea knows it.

Artie and Shea drive to Wessagussett Beach in Weymouth. Artie parks the truck and he and Shea climb down the long stairway (56 steps) to the rocky beach.

Artie scouted this area at low tide several weeks before.

There are two jetties, one long and one short. Artie's plan, worked out in consultation with Sandy Beach, is to start at the small jetty and work the outgoing tide to the tip of the larger jetty. Then, as the tide turns, work the same course in reverse. He plans to fish a fly called Lefty's Deceiver, which is a general baitfish imitation, unless the surface is dead calm, in which case he will switch to something that creates some surface commotion. He tells Shea the plan as he pulls on his waders. With his rod as his sword, his long-billed cap, polarized glasses, and anointed with sunscreen he feels very much the saltwater gladiator.

Shea has said scarcely a word, not wanting to infringe on Artie's need to concentrate. She sets up her chair in three inches of water and wishes him luck. She is reading *Beyond Yonder* by Stephen Morris, an allegory for the human species set in a small town in Vermont..

Artie notices that Sandy Beach is not speaking to him today and wonders if the presence of Shea has made him shy. He wades out to crotch level and works his line out to deep edge of the channel. Midway out to the longer jetty the familiar voice comes to him:

"You're showing off. You're thinking 'Damn, I look good,' but you're forgetting some key fishing basics. Did you see that you had a bass follow your fly just back there? But you did two things wrong. First you pulled your fly out of the water just when the fish was ready to strike. Remember, it's very important to fish each cast right to the very end. You've got to believe, every time you put your fly in the water, that you're going to catch a fish. You've got to believe. Secondly, you spooked the fish, because you retrieved the fly directly toward you. Remember when you're at about the twenty foot mark, move your retrieve off to the side to distract a fish from you. Your casts are fine. Damn, you do look good, and the babe on the beach is noticing."

Artie smiled at the ribbing from his mentor. Sandy was right. He was preening for Shea, and forgetting his fishing basics. By now Artie has worked out to the tip of the long jetty. Tide is nearly dead low. Artie sees a swirl near his fly. He can sense fish. The tide turns, imperceptibly at first, but within minutes he can sense the current strengthening. The breeze picks up noticeably.

A swirl, a hit. Artie's rod arcs as a frightened fish tries to swim to freedom. It's not a big fish, he can tell, but it's strong. He plays it in. About a sixteen-inch schoolie. Nice fish, but certainly not a keeper. He guides the fish to where he can grab it by the lower jaw. He takes it by the jaw and tail and lifts it out of the water, turning to show Shea. She's buried in her book, however, and misses the show. Slightly crestfallen, Artie returns the fish to the water and sways it back and forth in the water until its strength returns.

"Wind's come up." The gladiator has returned.

"Really, it seems delightful to me."

"Even casting into a light wind can be difficult. Did you see me catch the fish?"

"Oh no, I missed it. I am impressed with how graceful you are with your casting. Quite an improvement from when you started. You looked like poetry in motion out there."

"Yeah, I caught a nice fish out by the tip of that jetty just after the tide turned."

"Where is it?"

"Too small. Stripers have to be thirty inches long to keep. My goal for the summer is to catch just one legal fish."

"Are you all done?"

"Done fishing. Like I say, it's really hard casting into a head wind. We don't have to go now, though." Artie takes the suspenders off his shoulders and sits in the water next to Shea.

"So, tell me your story," he says. And like the gate on a spillway, a torrent of words poured forth.

I'm not sure why, but when Richard Mobien, started groping me in that elevator, my world crumpled. I worked hard to be in the express elevator heading to the 75th floor. I worked hard to be a peer of Richard Mobien. I did all the right things, only to be treated like an animal in a world where the only thing that counted was who was bigger and who was stronger. The worst part was, I respected the guy. I liked him. I trusted him. If he had asked me out on a date, I probably would have accepted. I've asked myself a million times, why did he do this? The only answer I can come up with is to show himself and me that he could.

Shea and Artie are still sitting in the waters of Wessagussett, but they've had to move three times due to the incoming tide. Tears are streaming down Shea's face. She's been talking for more than an hour. Artie has mostly murmured.

"One of the lessons I've learned," says Artie gently "is that we are all animals."

"I know. I know what you mean, but normal animals don't do to each other what Richard Mobien did to me. I put everything into my career. I didn't get married; I didn't have kids. All because I wanted to prove something, and above all I wanted to prove it to the Richard Mobiens of the world. I wanted to prove that I had arrived and that I belonged, he proved was that the President of Banque Suisse can make up his own rules."

She sobs. Artie touches her lightly on the arms and says that he's sorry.

The next day there is a stiff breeze, and the waters are too roiled to fish. Artie decides to scout out Thompson's Island. He asks Shea if she would like to come. They park the car and walk out over a gravel bar to the only privately owned island in Boston Harbor, now the site of an Outward Bound Education Center.

"So, you really did like *My Mother, My Lover...*?"

"I did," says Shea. "It helped me understand your pain."

"What! It wasn't about me." Artie doth protest too much. "It really is about this dicey issue of the changing roles of the sexes and how in a contemporaneous way..."

"Artie, I'm not interviewing you." They've reached the shore of Thompson's now. The backdrop of the Boston skyline looms behind them in stark contrast to the pastoral setting of the island. "You must have loved her very much."

"My Mother? Of course."

"I'm sure. I was referring to your wife."

"Evelyn? I don't know that I loved her so much as I was humiliated to be left not for another lover, but for a whole new lifestyle. I thought I had provided everything she wanted and needed."

They begin walking again. Shea says, "You know you really do have a lot of accumulated anger towards women." This opens the gate for Artie:

You know what really pisses me off. Bluebirds piss me off. All of my life bluebirds have been the symbol of happiness. And one of strong myths associated with bluebirds is that they mate for life. Of course the life span of a songbird is, what? Two years or something. Nevertheless, the image we were peddled is of a loving couple with mama and papa building the nest. They have little babies. Ma and Pa go off and collect bugs and stuff for the kids to eat. Pa defends the nest against predators, even huge monsters like crows and cats. But he's super bird, because he has the noble task of protecting his nest and his family. Well, I bought into that. Swallowed it hook, line, sinker, rod, reel...the whole damn deal. Now, it turns out the scientists have it wrong. After the first mating Pa builds the nest and Ma goes out and fucks every other horny bluebird stud she can find. The scientists say that this is adaptive behavior, because it expands the diversity of the gene pool. I say, fuck diversity. If I'm building the nest and protecting the young, I don't want to have my mate out there diversifying the gene pool. Why were we fed this lie that if we keep our noses clean, and stick to the straight and narrow, what results will be peace and harmony? Why didn't someone clue me in that it's all a lie?

"See where that salt pond is emptying into the bay?" They've been walking in silence following Artie's tirade. "I'll bet you stripers are waiting in the deeper water for baitfish to wash out. Tomorrow I'll cast my Lefty's Deceiver in there. Give it a little motion. And wham, I'll have a thirty-six incher on the line. We better head back before the gravel bar is covered, unless you want to spend the night out here."

So yes, on one level you are right. My Mother, My Lover…is all about me. But on another level it's about these stories and tunes that frame our worldview. What are we supposed to believe? Adam and Eve. I think I'm only now starting to understand the story. Adam was like this clueless guy who watched Monday Night Football, drank beer, scratched his balls, and generally was at peace with life. Eve comes along, and pretty soon he's got kids running around killing each other; his wife's probably out fucking bluebirds; and he's totally confused about life. It's like the schlub in My Mother, My Lover… He gives his whore of a sales manager a supportive hug, and before long he's living on a park bench where a bunch of teenagers set him on fire.

Angry. I'm not angry. I'm fucking livid. And I don't know where to go with it, because no matter how you slice it, I'm pretty lucky and it's my own damn fault!

The tide is just starting to cover the gravel bar. Shea and Artie cross as quickly as possible. Towards the end they are in a swift current up to their knees. On the way home they stop for fried clams and a creemee at a place not far from Howard Johnson's original ice cream stand. Without warning, Shea breaks down:

I don't know what I'm going to do! How can I go back to that office? How can I face those people? Even though people don't know what happened, I do. But I can't stay at Indian Mound, drinking herbal teas and meditating for the rest of my life. I wish I had kids, so I could interfere in their lives. I've thought of running away, but I like where I live. Maybe just changing careers would do it. My favorite client has always been the Massachusetts Bay Association. Maybe the world of non-profits and environmental stewardship will be different enough, but I don't know if I could survive in that world. Maybe I can start a little business, a gift shop or something. I don't know. I just don't know. I just know I can't go back.

They return to Indian Mound. They take turns taking showers in the outdoor shower overlooking the Boston Skyline that Nucking Fuff has devised. Then they go into Artie's bedroom and make love. Afterwards Artie leaks words like the cottage roof during a thunderstorm from the east.

I don't know what I'm going to do. Part of me wants to get back into the game and to show the same bastards who wrote me off that I'm a player. Then another part says "Fuck the system. You're beyond that. Make your own film, your own way, and if it works, reap the benefits. If it doesn't, so what? You've failed before.

Then, another part of me says take the money and run. You've seen how this system works. You've been a winner, and you've been a loser. You've been chewed up and spit out, and it's time to find more meaning in life than success. But suppose I make that point. I like being important. I like people hanging on my every word. I like swapping dirty jokes

*with Jack Nicholson at Laker games. I like having a crew of fifty and a
cast of thousands waiting for what I tell them to do.*

Artie takes a moment to look at Shea who returns his gaze
evenly. "You can't have it both ways," she says.

"And you like having twenty-something bimbos pretend
you're attractive," adds Shea.

"This is what you won't believe," says Artie. "They're not
pretending, because power is a real lubricant, an aphrodisiac. It
is exciting, and those who have it are attractive. What's-his-face
from Banque Suisse believed that."

"And What's-his-face was wrong!" She is angry.

"I'm sorry. That was unthinking of me. I was just trying to
make a point about power."

No Man Is An Island. Nomar Is A Shortstop

Artie calls Ike Frietag, the Sports Editor of *The Boston
Globe*:

*Mr. Frietag, my name is Arthur Gordon. We've never met, but you
may be familiar with some of my work as a filmmaker. I wrote and
directed* The King of California, Tails of Beyonder, *and, most
recently,* My Mother, My Lover *... you saw the video? Great! I won't
ask if you liked it.*

*The reason I'm calling has nothing to do with making films. I've
become very interested in fly fishing for striped bass in Boston Harbor,
and most of what I've learned has come from Sandy Beach. I tried to get
in touch with Mr. Beach, but I learned that 'Sandy Beach' is a pseudonym and that his forecasts, columns, and books are ghosted by Globe
staffers.*

No, I'm not calling you in any official capacity.

*No, I'm not representing any media. I'm just a guy trying to catch a
fish, and I happen to have become very interested in Sandy Beach.*

Lunch? I could do that. Wednesday will be fine. OK, the Globe cafeteria at 1 pm.

Ike Frietag is wearing a blue oxford shirt, no tie, dark chinos and running shoes. He is in his early forties, a fact betrayed only by the flecks of grey hair by his temples. He is trim, clean-shaven, and exactly where he told Artie he would be.

They greet each other and immediately get to a first-name basis. They make small talk on the way through the line. Frietag recommends the Philly cheese steak, then takes a taco salad for himself. Small talk in Boston usually involves the Red Sox. The question is never if they will break our hearts, but how. What fiendishly original way will they come up with to give us hope, then take it away?

At the table, Frietag takes a bite of his salad and then comes up with the requisite "So you're interested in Sandy Beach? I know this will strike you as unusual, but may I see some identification?"

"The last time I was asked was at the Quincy landfill, but at least they had a valid reason," says Artie who reaches to get his billfold and lets Frietag see his California driver's license.

"I need to be sure who I'm talking to," says Frietag, handing it back, "because, you see, I want to know about Sandy Beach, too."

I came here four years ago from Reuters news service where I was managing editor of the sports department. Big promotion for me. Like most of the people in the department, I'm most interested in the team sports-Red Sox, Patriots, Broons, Celtics. My job is to keep things running smoothly and to continually try to upgrade the accuracy of the reporting and the quality of the writing.

Fishing is of no personal interest to me, but it has an audience so it gets space in my section. Like a lot of the specialized subjects we deal with, we work with free-lancers and pay on a per word basis. I had been here two years, and I found myself reading Beach's Think Like a Fish column regularly. Suddenly it struck me. I've never ok'd a payment to Sandy Beach.

I do a little research, and as you might I expect, I find a secretary who has been at the Globe since whenever and who knows a lot more about my department than I do. Apparently there was a Sandy Beach who wrote a fishing column for us back in the 1960s. The guy died and someone came up with the idea of continuing the column under his name, which was a pseudonym anyway. We also had the little charicature of Beach that we use as kind of a logo.

It continued this way until in the early 1980s someone began sending in area fishing reports, and their reports were much better than our own, which were generated by having an intern call around to various bait and tackle shops. This person obviously knew the harbor like the back of his hand. The material would arrive, always meeting deadline, in a plain envelope with no return address. The writer asked for no payment and provided no contact information. After a few years, Beach started sending in material relating to the deteriorating water quality in Boston Harbor. The writing was quite good, very impassioned, and generated a very favorable reader response. Luckily, politicians read the sports pages and Beach's message was heard.

Of course, the Globe's policy today is to never accept material without attribution, but things weren't so formal back then. Beach's material evolved into his Think Like a Fish column, and it's been a sports page fixture ever since.

I can understand how something like this could slide into place. It didn't affect the budget negatively. Beach's material is always well prepared, on time, and rarely controversial, at least these days.

So this was the situation in place when I took the job, and nobody clued me in. Why should they? If it ain't broke, why fix it?

Originally the material was mailed in a plain envelope with no return address. Then for a few years it came via fax, and now it comes via email from sandybeach@hotmail.com . *I don't know who this guy is, where he lives, or how he gets his information, but he does a good job of it.*

I made an effort to contact Beach. At first I claimed that we were getting personal appearance requests that we wanted to pass along, but all these generated was an email explanation about how Beach wants to protect his privacy so that people don't bother him when he is fishing. Then I tried a more heavy-handed approach, and said that the Globe now had a policy of no anonymous submissions and that if Beach did not supply personal contact info, including his social security number, that we would discontinue his forecasts and column. No response, but when I brought it up at our editorial meeting, everyone agreed we were shooting ourselves in the foot. Sandy Beach is pretty popular with readers, and no one can match his encyclopedic knowledge of the harbor.

Plus, no one on the staff wanted to pick up the slack. Also, from a personal perspective, I didn't want to be the bad guy to explain to irate readers that we were using bureaucratic bullshit to invade the privacy of a popular columnist . It's not as if readers care about who is or isn't Sandy Beach. They just want to know where to go to catch fish.

So, Beach called our bluff and we blinked. We swallowed our journalistic integrity and keep using his stuff. And everyone's happy. Even me, although I am curious as hell to meet this guy.

This situation is known by area fishermen, who have a great time speculating about Sandy Beach's true identity.

Freitag and Artie complete their lunch brainstorming on ways they can identify Sandy Beach. Artie tells him what his studios research department turned up. After a few futile ideas are exchanged, they go back to musing about whether or not this will be the year the Red Sox can beat the Yanks. Artie has one last question:

"Do you know the original Sandy Beach's real name?"

"I have no idea," says Frietag.

Chapter 8 - Bluebirds!

When Artie checks his messages there is one from Elaine. Sony Pictures has announced that they are putting *My Mother, My Lover...* back into theatrical release, opening on 1200 screens nationally. According to the trades, this is to signal the Academy of Motion Pictures that they think the picture deserves serious consideration for an Oscar. Universal has jumped in on the bidding for the sequel, and has jumped the bid to ten million plus two points of gross. Gross, for chrissakes, Arthur, gross, bleats Elaine. Artie calls he back to say he still hasn't made up his mind, but he feels himself getting closer.

Chapter 9 - ANd bEcAUse we cAN!

Sandy Beach's Fishing Forecast for September

There's the good news and the bad news. The cooler water can energize the bass and perk up their appetites. There's far less traffic on the water, and fewer idiots roaring around on jet skies. The smelt come in, and sometimes you can have fun taking a break from bass if you encounter a school of smelt. It can be fun to watch them scatter from a big, scary fly. The bigger fish seem to linger a bit longer, meaning your solitude can be shattered at any moment by a boisterous bull of a bass.

But the colder water means the wading becomes progressively less comfortable. You can compensate by wearing more layers of clothing, but that carries its own set of risks, especially if you take a header.

Even when it's warm and sunny, there's a tinge of sadness just knowing that the fish are leaving. It's not unlike the feeling of going back to school after Labor Day. It's just a transition, but transitions aren't things that fisherfolk handle well.

Watch the moon. Fish the strongest tides, especially when they happen at daybreak and dusk. As the days grow shorter, so will chances of catching The Big One. That's really bad news.

-Sandy Beach, from *The Boston Globe*

Labor Day

Labor Day came early, September 2. As a young boy, when Indian Mound was still a colony of cottages, this was both Artie's favorite and least favorite day of the year. In the morning there would be a ceremonial raising of the flag by the waterfront. Some old person would rattle a drum, or for a few years Cuzzin blatted a trumpet. Then, while the adults sipped coffee and munched on coffeecake, the kids engaged in feats of prowess and dominance-foot races, three-legged races, egg tosses, sack races. Artie took these very seriously and always came away with his share of prizes, but so did everyone else, he eventually realized. For a few hours it was like the Fourth of July all over again, but whereas on the Fourth the celebration continued as if summer would never end with water races, a costume parade, a potluck dinner, and even dancing on the waterfront, on Labor Day the festivities ended abruptly. Moms were in a fit of packing. Dads were boarding up cottages that were filled with light and life just a day before. People said their good-byes.

Until next year.

But then came the road, and the cars, and the pavement, and adolescence, and the assassination of JFK, and Vietnam. Even worse kids started going back to school before Labor Day!

In future years, no matter where he was, L.A. or on a set somewhere, Artie always tracked Labor Day, and it always made him feel the same, and he could never quite explain the feelings. Each year he died a little on Labor Day, but it was such a pleasant death.

Tracking shot. The people leaving Indian Mound, as seen from behind. The super hero-a young, seemingly average-looking boy-uses his powers to accelerate the rotation of the earth so that fall, winter, and spring are condensed into a nano-second, and it's the dawn of summer again.

"Pretty fucking lame," Artie says to himself. "Why did they wreck the world, all in the name of progress?"

This is the first year he has stayed at the cottage in September. The first two weeks are sheer delight. It's quiet. Things have settled in for a different season. Liam has returned from L.A. and is back at Berklee. He has already announced that he will be going back to L.A. when he finishes the semester in January. He and Mieko are starting a band. Elaine has come out again from the Coast, ostensibly to talk with Artie about the stalled negotiation. This time she stays with Cuzzin who is blue with the non-status of his restaurant.

Artie and Shea are sleeping together every night. In August they are exclusively in the cottage. As September progresses they migrate to Shea's.

Estherina

The hurricane season runs officially from June 1 to November 30. No one pays much attention until after Labor Day. Estherina is the fifth hurricane of the season. It forms as a tropical depression off the west coast of Africa, gathers strength across the Horse Latitudes, socks the hell out of Bermuda, then spends a couple of days idling before making a leisurely bee line for Indian Mound. With top winds of 255 kilometers per hour, it's hard to think of any aspect of the storm as "leisurely," but it moves at the pace of a fast walk or a slow trot (you can't have it both ways) up the Gulf Stream.

The residents of eastern Massachusetts have ample warning. When Artie goes to The Depot, he finds Atherton, his favorite Department Manager out straight, connecting people with duct tape, plywood, generators, gas cans, chain saws, flashlights, water containers, and batteries. There's a sense of excitement and purpose in the air, just as there is when the Red Sox are still in the pennant race.

"You going to board up your cottage?" he asks Artie.

"Naw. The place has lasted through a hundred years of hurricanes. If its time has come, its time has come."

"But this is a Category Five hurricane! This is a monster. Andrew caused $30 billion in damage back in 1992. Mitch killed 10,000 in the Caribbean."

"How much of that $30 billion ended up flowing into the registers at The Depot?" asks Artie.

"A lot. We have special merchandise selections for this time of year. Look at all these people. It's a feeding frenzy."

"Well, I just need you to feed me some duct tape."

"No kidding, Mr. Gordon, you're not planning to stay at the cottage through this storm?" At the note of concern in Atherton's voice, Artie pauses. This kid has seen him through gardening, painting, and every botched project in between. Now, he's concerned about his safety. Artie is suddenly over-whelmed with gratitude, nostalgia, and affection.

"Yes, I am," he changes tone. "I didn't do all this work just to see the cottage get blown away. And if it does, I want to go with it. Atherton, I want to thank you for all your help these past months, all your answers to my stupid questions. I really do have a friend at The Depot."

"I dunno. You don't want to take any chances with Estherina. She's a Category Five, and they're saying she's going to hit at high tide and during the full moon."

"It's still nearly a week away. They can't predict these things that accurately. I do appreciate your concern, really. I'll be all right."

"Hey, I finally saw your movie."

"Didja like it?"

"Not really. Didn't have enough action or sex."

The residents of Pissiwagassett tape their windows with masking tape, and pull the few remaining boats from the Bay, but no one evacuates. Five days have passed since Artie's trip to The Depot and Estherina has evolved from legend to real. Now, the storm is predicted to hit at mid-day and at low tide, meaning that flooding will probably not be serious. Everyone draws extra water and readies the candles and food, but the overall attitude is now drama and anticipation, not fear and horror.

Shea lobbies for them to be together at her house, but when he repeats his determination to stay at the cottage, she agrees to join him.

Estherina does not disappoint. She sweeps in by mid-morning with a blast of tropical air and horizontal rain. Artie, Shea, and several others go to the beach to experience the awesome power first hand, but a falling branch reminds them that Mother Nature neither provides entertainment nor plays games. Everyone scurries back to protection.

"Protection" is perhaps an overstatement of what the cottage provides. "Veneer" is a more apt word. The wooden frame groans during the gusts. The chaos outside is barely kept at bay. By ten a.m. the power has been lost. Even Artie's cell phone is mercifully inoperative.

"Want to fool around?" says Shea.

"I'm astounded by the way your mind works," says Artie.

"If you knew what's really on my mind, you'd really be astounded."

"I'm sure I will find out soon enough."

Shea removes her t-shirt with a flourish. She is wearing no bra. Artie takes her in visually and, in the true spirit of American manhood, says simply "ok."

They are standing in the middle of the living room of the

cottage. She embraces him and they kiss passionately. Under other circumstances they might have been sensitive to the prospect of a neighbor seeing in or dropping by, but enveloped in the womb of Estherina, they feel safe.

Shea slides down Artie's body, tugging on his belt, then pulling his trousers and underwear down to his ankles. Quickly, she goes to one knee, then two, taking his penis into her mouth and sucking on him until his entire brain has descended. Then, she pulls back, keeping a strong hand on his manhood.

"Jesus," murmurs Artie, returning briefly to the planet. "This is what you had in mind?"

"Even better," she says, staring directly into the eye of his penis, then running her tongue along the bottom of his shaft. "Now, I'm going to feed you grapes." Abruptly she stands, releases his penis, and walks into the kitchen.

"Am I supposed to stand here?" asks Artie, suddenly feeling slightly foolish.

"Meet me at the couch, she says, returning with a bunch of grapes. She pushes aside the small coffee table in front of the couch, and removes her clothes and underpants in a single motion. "And why don't you make yourself comfortable?" She goes to Artie, takes his penis gently in her hand, and pulls him toward the couch. With his ankles shackled by his trousers, however, Artie can manage only baby steps.

"Do you want me to lie with my head in your lap?"

"Actually, I'm going to make you work a little harder for these grapes." Shea sits on the couch and draws her knees up to her chest. She pucks a single bright green grape from the bunch, puts it briefly in her mouth, then pulls it out with a thumb and forefinger and inserts it in her vagina.

"You washed these, I hope," she says.

"Oh yeah," says Artie. "Plus, they're organic."

"OK, then, 'Mangia!'" she says.

"Why are we doing this?" asks Artie, standing before her, staring into her crotch.

"Because it feels good. Because it's fun. Because we're adults, and because we can," she responds. Artie falls to his knees and begins to probe her with his tongue. Shea begins soft murmurs of pleasure.

"Got it!" says Artie, softly, but with enthusiasm.

She holds up her bunch of grapes, places another one in her mouth, and says "One down and about a hundred to go."

After the fifth grape, Shea pulls Artie up gently into her horizon. "Now, Arthur, I want you to bone me good."

Artie does as he is told, thrusting himself into her. She urges him on with a crescendo of pants that climaxes in an almost blood-curdling orgasm for her. But for the roar and chaos of Estherina are Shea's moans and release as silent as the tree falling in the forest.

Artie, who has been exerting copious amounts of energy, withdraws and kneels with his head resting on her stomach.

"You're not giving up, are you?" asks Shea.

"Yeah, I've had enough for the moment," he says, still gulping breaths. "That was quite a performance."

"That was the best orgasm of my life," she says. "Don't you want to cum off?"

"It's really not necessary."

"Of course you want to cum off. I insist."

"You can't insist that I cum off."

"No, but I can make myself irresistible." Shea pushes Artie's head down towards her groin and clasps him to her pelvis. "You can't resist those pheromones," she says with a playful tone. "It's just like with those horseshoe crabs. You poor, dumb males don't stand a chance."

Shea pushes Artie away and turns over, leaning her forearms on the back of the sofa and wiggling her behind seductively. She speaks in a pouty little voice designed to provoke:

"Oooo, is de big bull striper going to spread his milt over de wittle girl striper?"

"I've never seen this side of you. You really are kind of a slut."

"What if de wittle girl striper wiggles her wittle tale, kind of like this. Now is de big bull striper going to squirt his milt? Or is de big bull striper going to let de wittle girl striper swim away so that some other big bull striper can spread his milt over her."

Artie grabs her firmly by the hips and enters her. He speaks to no one in particular in single words that escape between clenched teeth. "No.... big, bull striper....gonna do the mandatory ... gonna do whatever ...gonna do you ... BecauSe I Am the kINg... thE KINGdoM ... THe PoweR ... THE glORY ... beCAuse IT fEEls goOD ... BeCaUsE it's FuN ... beCUZ wE'Re ADuLTs ... ANd bEcAUse we cAN!."

As he climaxes, spilling himself into her, he sees his own reflection in the glass of a framed picture of a whaling scene. He sees a middle-aged man, with a slight potbelly, thinning grey hair that sprouts randomly around his body, now shouting incoherently while clutching ferociously to the hips of a woman who would not, could not, will not, cannot be denied. As his ejaculation ends, the couple becomes still, quietly remembering that they are in the midst of Hurricane Estherina.

"Good job, Captain," says Shea, turning over and holding out her arms.

Artie falls into them gently, willingly. He is slightly surprised to hear himself saying "I love you."

Outside, Estherina tries to pry the roof off the cottage.

Fried Onion Rings

Bull Gordon always maintained that the onion ring was the best backdrop for evaluating a cook's prowess, much as the ice cream maker's reputation must rest on their ability to make vanilla ice cream. When Bull cruised the car hops and drive-ins of coastal New England. He'd always make his initial assessment by ordering onion rings.

"Onion rings are so simple that a thousand things can go wrong. Start with the onion. Texture is all important. You want an onion that is dense and hard. Next is uniformity. It hard to ever do justice to different sizes in the same basket.

"Soak the onions in a large bowl of cold water. You'll need a separate fry mix, and the range of styles is infinite. Some people like a bready mix, but in my opinion this overpowers the onion and all you taste is the coating. I like my mix light and crisp, providing the maximum contrast with the spicy onion and not overpowering it. Sift together these ingredients:

- *Flour*
- *Non-fat powdered milk*
- *Bicarbonate of soda*
- *Salt*
- *Powdered egg whites*

Take a double fistful of onions from the water, give it two big shakes, drop the onions in the fry mix. Wipe your hand on your apron. Toss the onions until they are evenly coated. Don't worry about making a mess. You're going to. Put the onions into the fat. You don't have to use a sepa-

rate fryer for onions if you are using a Gordon's Fat Filtron®.

Onions will spatter due to the high moisture content. Cook only about one minute, or until golden brown. Listen to the grease. The onions will tell you when they are done. Drain onto paper towels. Two shakes of salt from the industrial shaker. Perfect!"

Deer Island

Shea is having a morning cup of tea, reading the Boston Globe, with the morning news on the background television. It's a warm day in late September, the kind you have to cling to, the kind that gets you through the winter.

Her attention goes exclusively to the television when a familiar face appears on the screen and she hears:

"At a press conference yesterday a group of Wampanoag Indians, led by Chief Joe Liquordup produced what they say is documentation to a claim to Deer Island, site of the state-of-the-art Sanitation Facility completed in the year 2000. According to Liquordup, the land was forcefully taken from the Wampanoags in 1685, in violation of a treaty signed just five years earlier, that gave them the land in perpetuity for use as a burial ground."

Cut to Joe: "We just want what is lawfully ours. We want our property and our dignity restored."

Back to announcer: "The group will march on Deer Island later today to perform ritual dances to honor their ancestors. Officials of the Wampanoags would neither confirm nor deny that they plan to open a gambling casino on Deer Island."

Shea smiles and speaks to the television "So we were your warm-up act, the shakedown cruise. Say hi to Artie."

Shea says this because Artie is at this moment enroute to

Deer Island. Inspired by Sandy Beach's latest forecast in The Boston Globe he has driven north of Boston to fish some recommended locations. He is running out of summer. He hasn't achieved his goal of catching a legal striper, and within weeks the fish, most of them anyway, will be heading to warmer water.

He leaves early enough to beat the rush hour traffic and takes the Ted Williams Tunnel onto Route 1A. He goes past Logan Airport and drives through the cramped streets of East Boston. After years in L.A. with its endless freeways, access roads, and on ramps, this ethnic potpourri seems otherworldly. "Where are the fast-food chains?" he wonders.

He turns onto Shirley Street, following a sign to the Deer Island Sanitation Facility. East Boston morphs into Winthrop-By-The-Sea, a Victorian relic that seems getting ready to be rediscovered. It's oddly familiar to Artie. At the age of ten or so, he would occasionally accompany his Uncle Bull and his cousin Cuzzin on Bull's trips to the fried food emporiums. In addition to Howard Johnson's and Dunkin Donuts, Bull sold his Gordon Filtrons® to Mom & Pop drive-ins and clam shacks. It's déjà vu for Artie. He's cruising streets that he cruised, perhaps once, more than forty years ago, igniting small and well-buried images and emotions with each passing block.

He begins to catch glimpses of the ocean in between the converted cottages. Every inch of ground has been paved or built upon, like a larger Indian Mound. Artie is a South Shore kinda guy, with a South Shore orientation towards the landmarks of Boston Harbor. He feels as if he is on the wrong side of the world. All the landmarks are there-the Prudential, the Custom House, Long Island Bridge, Boston Light-but in reverse frame.

Deer Island, like most of the islands in Boston Harbor, is a whore to humanity, with a colorful, checkered past featuring great storms, heroic characters, despicable villains, and unspeakable beauty.

Islands and humans typically have wary relationships. Islands, for the technically minded, are pieces of land surrounded by water. They are beautiful, romantic, idyllic and hopelessly exploited. Islands are where society puts things that need to be contained. Islands, for instance, are good places to put convicts, because the sea saves the work of building fences that never work quite well enough.

Diseased people, too, are good to put on islands, as well as the deformed, the impoverished, the insane, unwed pregnant mothers, and the eccentric of all varieties and flavors.

Islands are also good place to stage the forbidden, the societal definitions of which change from decade to decade. Prostitution, gambling, prize fighting, cock fighting, and dog fights are all activities more suited to islands than downtowns, and all, at one time or another, have thrived on the islands of Boston Harbor.

Hm-m-m. Gambling.

Islands are also good places to dump any of society's waste, whether it is of the excremental variety or the truckloads of dirt from The Big Dig.

The ecosystems of islands are fragile and easily altered. Deer Island's has been so thoroughly blasted to smithereens that there is no telling what it was like originally. The first things to go were the trees. Those early English colonists loved to denude the landscape. After stripping the wood, they would bring grazing animals, generally sheep, to make sure the forests stayed away. They also, wittingly and otherwise, introduced species like rats and cats, that thrive on the island to this day.

You Can't Have It

Deer Island, because of its proximity to Boston and ease of access, has been perhaps the premier waste repository in Boston Harbor. It is now connected to the mainland by a causeway. As the residents of Indian Mound have learned, the umbilical to the mainland comes with its own price.

Artie parks in a small access lot. He puts on his waders and selects flies for the day. He walks towards the eastern side of island. It's mid-afternoon on a perfect day. His plan is to spend a few hour scouting, then to start fishing approximately two hours before the low tide at 6:46 pm. The days have grown shorter, and it will be approaching dusk. The water temperature, he notes, is almost ten degrees cooler that it was in mid-August.

He enters the water near an exposed mussel bed on the south side of Deer Island. The rocks are round and slippery, coated with a greasy moss. In front of him, only a mile away, is Logan Airport, with two active runways, and planes stacked up as far as the eye can see. He watches a Lufthansa 747 touch down, followed by a colorful jet from Southwest.

"Welcome to Beantown," he mutters.

He releases his fly and tries a few short casts, then strips out more line and begins working his way out one step per cast. It will take him about thirty minutes to work his way out to the end of the exposed point. This will put him at the furthermost point at dead low. He will then work his way back on the incoming.

A cargo ship, its decks piled with colorful containers, seemingly close enough to touch, passes before him, heading for the open ocean. Destination unknown, although Artie can read the home port of Liberia on the stern. Numerous other small craft are playing about, as everyone wants to cling to the last gasp of nice weather. The white sails contrast gaily with the blue waters, while the distant skyline is settled in shadow, backlit by the descending sun.

Impressed as he is by the panorama, Artie is thinking like a fish. There are birds about, but nothing is actively working the surface. Artie can sense stripers lurking just beyond the drop off to deeper water.

"These guys need something to wake them up," Sandy Beach tells him. "They're fat, dumb, and happy from gorging all summer. Try a Crab Gurgler and make as much noise as you can."

The Gurgler is a surface fly that plows through the water with the grace of a drunk Bruins fan. "What I don't understand," says Artie, "is how a Crab Gurgler can work. Crabs are creatures of the bottom. A crab on the surface makes no sense whatsoever."

"Don't argue with your guru," says Beach. "Try the Crab Gurgler. Sometimes a bass just needs to be provoked."

Artie can't see it, but several hundred yards behind him, the view blocked by a steep slope of granite blocks and a seawall built to fend off the North Atlantic, rise the massive "eggs" of the wastewater treatment plant. Here more than one billion gallons of water containing the body wastes of more than two million people passes daily. The sewage arrives through four massive tunnels, more than one hundred feet underground. Massive pumps lift the sewage into primary treatment clarifiers where scum is removed from the surface by giant skimmers and sludge that settles at the bottom is pumped out for removal to a landfill.

The remaining liquid is then pumped into one of the twelve, 140 foot tall egg-shaped anaerobic digesters, where additional organic matter is consumed through a biological process that mimics the fermentation that occurs naturally in the stomach. After "digestion" what remains are methane gas, carbon dioxide, water, and solid organic byproducts. The methane is burned to provide power for the plant. The solids are barged to a plant not far from Indian Mound where it is pelletized into a fertilizer product. The carbon dioxide is released into the atmosphere. The water is sanitized with sodium hypochlorite, then dechlorinated with sodium bisulfite before being discharged into a 24 foot diameter, 100 foot deep tunnel that runs 9.5 miles out into Massachusetts Bay.

Nine point five miles!

The digesters dwarf the score of Wampanoags beating drums and dancing at their base. The dancers are greatly outnumbered by onlookers, most of whom are carrying cameras. A tiny Joe Liquordup, wearing his full headdress, is surrounded by people asking questions and taking notes.

Cast, step, cast, step. Artie feels his way along the slippery bottom. He is in water that comes just over his balls, which is how he knows that the temperature is ten degrees cooler than a month earlier. "I am blessed," he says "to be living in this world of fish."

A United jet, laden with businessmen, streams in from Chicago, followed by an Aer Lingus 707 from Shannon. A party boat, with a live Dixieland band, approaches. Its top deck is heavy with Japanese men wearing identical dark suits who are doing their collective best to drink too much. The boat comes so close that Artie thinks he can reach it with a perfect cast. The people on board wave and shout in Japanese.

The tide is now dead low. There is only an instant of stillness, then he feels the current moving in the opposite direction, pulled by the moon. He is on plan. He begins to fish the opposite side of the bar. Step, cast, gurgle, gurgle. He is buoyed by the spectacle before him, the birds and planes overhead, the boats on the water, the striped bass just below, the people in the skyscrapers shitting and pissing, their wastes passing many feet beneath him enroute to sanitization and the 9.5 mile flush into the Atlantic.

Within the next few seconds several important events take place. A 42 inch striped bass approaches Artie's Crab Gurgler, its gaping mouth seemingly wide enough to engulf Deer Island. Artie sees it perfectly. A commuter ferry passes by, its occupants deep in thoughts of workaday events and waiting martinis. And Artie steps into a hole. Although the hole is less than two feet deep, it completely upsets his balance. Just as he feels the first desperate flight of a fish attached to him by the thinnest strand of transparent line, his feet lose contact with the bottom and there is water everywhere-in his eyes, in his nose, in his lungs, and in his waders. He hand sets the hook just before submerging. As he goes down, he hangs on to his fly rod and inhales a lungful of salt water.

Now, there is an abrupt cut, as if the director doesn't mind you being momentarily confused.

Artie is, without explanation or warning, now sitting on the granite blocks that line the southern shore of Deer Island. Even though it is dusk, the blocks retain the warmth from baking in the sun all day. He's dry and tranquil. Next to him is the woman he met on the mudflats near Indian Mound who introduced him to fly fishing.

"Hi Arthur. You've gotten pretty good at fly fishing." She's casual, inviting. Artie knows he should be confused, but he's not.

"I don't know about the 'fishing' part, but I'm definitely better at the 'fly" part. I had a good teacher in Sandy Beach."

"A teacher is only as good as the student's willingness to learn. Looks like you've gotten yourself into a bit of a situation," she says, gesturing to the water.

Artie looks out to see himself struggle to his feet, his right arm holding his bent fly rod high. He's hacking violently from the ingestion of sea water. Just as it looks as if he will reach vertical, the wake from the ferry knocks him below the surface again.

Artie looks to the woman. It's Cassie, right?"

"That's right. Cassandra, Cassandra Arthur." She offers her hand. Artie takes it numbly. "Are you familiar with the mythological Cassandra?" she asks.

Artie looks at her face intently. He's never seen a human visage so radiant, so inviting. "Something to do with the Trojan horse?"

"I'll give you partial credit. Cassandra was blessed by the gods with the ability to foresee the future, but equally cursed by the same gods who then made it so that no one would believe her. There's more to it, but that's the executive summary, because you don't have time."

"And why's that?"

She points to the water. Artie sees himself flailing to find his footing, gasping and choking, but still holding his fly rod. "You're drowning, in case you've forgotten."

"Are you an angel or something?"

"I'm definitely something, and you can either ask questions or you can decide what to do."

Artie watches himself flail the water. He is less than four feet of water, but between the slippery rocks, the waves, and the current, he can't seem to get vertical.

"Does anyone ever call you 'Sandy?'"

"No one does, but they could."

"And might you be related to a certain Gordon Arthur?"

She nods. "My Dad."

"Does your being here have anything to do with his death?"

"More questions. OK, here's how I see it. You're only in four feet of water. There's no way you should drown, but at the moment you're in a world of hurt. You've lost your equilibrium; you're gasping for breath; you don't realize it, but you're actually in the early stages of hypothermia, because so much of your body heat has leached out into the cool water; the current and slippery footing are working against you; and to make everything worse, your priority is to hold on to that fly rod."

"I really want to catch that fish. That's become my cause in life."

"I think that's what happened to my father. I think he was concentrating so hard on fishing that he forgot about living, but I'm much better at seeing the future than the past. That's part of my curse." Artie had never been in the presence of such composure, such equanimity.

"So, do I catch the fish, or drown trying?" he asks.

"I don't know. Could go either way. Or, you could catch it and find out you've caught a bluefish, or even a dogfish."

"Oh no, it was a striper. I saw it."

"OK, so you could catch the fish and get killed by a drunk driver on the Southeast Expressway. Who knows? My point is that you are currently floundering. If you don't decide something soon, you'll have no choice to make. That's my whole point in being here, to tell you you've got a choice, and to say you can't have it both ways."

Shea has prepared a late dinner, and brought it over to the cottage. She has lit several candles and placed them strategically. She can't wait to tell Artie about the Wampanoag demonstration on Deer Island. Maybe he'll have a first-hand account.

She knows enough not to expect punctuality from a man who goes to the sea in search of fish, but there comes a time when it is too dark to fish. That time came and went two hours ago. It takes less than half an hour to drive from Deer Island back to Indian Mound. He should be home. She blows out the candles and tries to distract herself with a book. She's an hour and a half worried.

When she finally hears a noise on the front porch it is past ten. She's unnerved, "Artie?"

The door opens and a pasty, near naked, bedraggled Arthur Gordon staggers in.

"Omigod," screams Shea. "What happened to you? Are you all right?"

The story comes out in incoherent spurts, complete with jets, ferries, skyscrapers, giant bass with gaping mouths, and Cassandra Gordon, also known as Sandy Beach. Artie had to spend almost an hour in the truck with the heater going to get his body temperature back to normal. Yes, he saw the Wampanoags, even Joe. They marched by while he was shivering in the truck. He lost his rod. A giant striper is dragging it around Boston Harbor. Yes, I'm kidding. I'm sure the leader broke. He almost drowned in three feet of water. Do you know about the Trojan Horse?

Elaine, it's Artie. Yes, I've decided. I've thought through the independent route, but whenever I think of having to raise millions of dollars, I get sick. Let's sell to Spielberg and be done with it. We need at least six million dollars-two for the government, one for you, one to blow on Cuzzin's restaurant, and two to get me through the rest of life. Do your best and then come back out here and we'll celebrate. You can stay at the cottage, even though it's getting a little nippy. Or....you can make your own arrangements.

(continued from page 100)

What's For Dessert? The Dessert Debate, Part II

"You've got to have great desserts."

"I've got it covered."

"Not fried Indian Pudding."

"I actually tried that, and it was good, but a little much after fish & chips and fried onion rings. It was hard to tell where the pudding left off and the fried crust begins."

"What are your great desserts?"

"Ice cream."

"Ice cream?"

"Well, not exactly ice cream. You know, the soft stuff. Dairy Queen. Soft-serve. Creamee. Whatever."

"You mean the stuff that comes out of a machine only in vanilla and chocolate."

"I'm only serving vanilla."

"That's it?"

"Not exactly. You can get it with fresh strawberries, fresh peaches, fresh blueberries, or Cuzzin's Famous Hot Fudge Sauce that you can also buy to-go in jars."

"That's your entire dessert menu?"

"We'll also offer fresh watermelon in season."

"Hm-m-m. In your own way you do have it covered."

"32 pieces of melon per, at $2 a slice, equals $64 per melon."

"Do you make money on the ice cream?"

"75 servings a day, buck-fifty a serving, cost of goods eighteen cents. That's nearly a hundred bucks a day of profit, more if you factor in the fruit and hot fudge."

Part 4
These Days
Epilogue

Sandy Beach's Column for April

April is the cruelest month, at least for the wading salt water fly fisherman. The water is so cold that it numbs your legs no matter how many layers you wear. Your hands fumble and mis-tie even familiar knots. There are no fish around yet, but you know they are coming. In the winter you can stare at maps and charts and plot strategies. You can tie flies and picture their action perfectly in your mind. But now, the weather is no longer so bad that you can live inside your fantasies. You have to go outside and start flogging the water, but there are no fish, and the water is so @#$%##!! cold.

-Sandy Beach, from *The Boston Globe*

Interview with Liam Gordon in The Wrong Note, *a guide to the L.A. music scene*

Q. So why didn't you just become a famous film director like your dad?

A. I will, when I'm finished being a rock star.

Q. How did your band get its name, Nucking Fuff?

A. That's actually a tough question, because we are playing with themes on both sociological and religious levels. I was listening to The Who's *Won't Get Fooled Again*. Remember the last line, "Meet the new boss, same as the old boss?" I started playing around with the concept of the "new king," instead of "new boss," which led me to two obvious places-Elvis and Jesus. I kept thinking, "What's the connection?" And eventually I came to the point that Jesus is really Elvis, but without the fluff. So what's Elvis without the fluff? It's what's real and legitimate and authentic, like the manger on Christmas Eve, when the three wise men arrive. Then it hit me. What's Elvis without the fluff? Christmas. Noel. What's "fluff" with "no-el," fuff. Nucking Fuff was born.

Q. That's incredible. Is it true?

A. Not a word of it. It's just a pretentious little affectation from a snotty musician. The name came to our base player, Leif, in a dream.

Q. Let's move on. It's an over-used phase, but would you call your new CD *The Battle of Indian Mound* a theme album?

A. I'd rather call it a "good album," but if people want to see a central theme in it, that's fine, too. There are some obvious musical elements that carry over from song to song. For instance the same chord progression is used in the chorus for *Move It a C-Hair*, *The Size of Your Dick*, and *Spray It White*, although the words and melody are entirely different. I hope this doesn't sound too ambitiously technical, but what I'm hoping to accomplish is a sense of stability and constancy in a world that appears to be always changing.

Q. Did it change the dynamic to bring a female

lead singer into the group?

A. Change the dynamic? "Obliterate" the dynamic is more like it. A song like *Chink Bimbo* comes across as mean-spirited and cynical when sung by me. When Meiko sings it, it's funny.

Q. Your lyrics have been criticized by some feminists, who point to lyrics like the line in *Garden Bitch* where you say *"You're a perennial pain in my ass."* Are you a sexist?

A. Absolutely, and proudly so.

Q. And yet you come up with a tender, sentimental ballad like *Estherina*. Who inspired that?

A. Estherina? That would be my Mother. Mother Nature, that is.

Q. And what about *You Can't Have It Both Ways*? There's a song with multiple layers of meaning. How would you summarize it for us?

A. It's about sex, pure and simple. You can really only *do it* in one position at a time, so you have to make a choice. On top, on the bottom, in front, behind, upside down....you have to make a choice. I guess you could say that the theme of this song is commitment.

Q. What comes next for Nucking Fuff?

A. We're doing a tour of college campuses, promoting *The Battle of Indian Mound*. One of the highlights will be a concert at the Berklee School of Music that I just (barely) graduated from. We're also doing a private gig at my father's wedding in April.

Stripah Love

It's a bright April day that reminds you what spring is about. It's a day when forsythia is the most beautiful color in the world. A giant crane is at the corner of Ocean Avenue and Germantown Pike lowering a fifteen foot long, fiberglass striped bass onto the roof of Cuzzin's Seafood, The Home of Fried Sushi. Bright signage, reflecting Cuzzin's hand-scrawled humor says "Grand Opening Arpil 16(intentional misspellings). Spend your tax refund on a Clambake with Cuzzin."

The man himself is watching from the sidewalk, not far from where Artie stood paralyzed a year earlier. With him is Elaine. Her transition is complete. She is now a disheveled, female counterpart. She wears a bandana and a jean jacket that was used to wash the parking lot. She has gained a few pounds, but seems entirely comfortable in her skin. Their "his and hers" Harleys are parked side by each alongside the building.

Elaine and Cuzzin have formed a partnership that is based on a foundation of mutual abuse. To an outsider they appear to be fighting viciously. Cuzzin will call her an "ugly, fuckin', syphilitic whore" and she will respond by threatening "pull his cock out so far she'll be able to wrap it around his neck and strangle him."

Let anyone come between them, however, and their bile will become instantly galvanized onto the intruder. Having observed the foul intercourse repeatedly, Artie is content to muse to Shea "Add this to the list of things I don't understand in life."

Cuzzin has changed appearance again. "Gotta look like a restaurantoowah." He says. His head is now shaved save for two gray patches on the back of his head that grow down to the nape of his neck. He has grown the world's longest mustache that creeps around his mouth, down to the line of his jaw, and then four tangled inches beyond. He looks like a cross between a pirate and a Salvador Dali dream. And he looks happy.

The parking lot has been cleaned up, covered with

crushed shells, and handsomely landscaped, with picnic tables with brightly colored umbrellas overlooking the now visible salt marsh. Cars stream by. Many honk. Cuzzin stands on the sidewalk and waves like a politician. He is on a cell phone with a built-in digital camera. He's talking with his nephew, Liam, now a fledgling rock star in L.A., showing him live photos of the fish going into place. Liam sends a photo of himself. Meiko is on his arm. She sends her love. They promise to visit for a few days when Nucking Fuff comes to play Berklee.

Artie drives up in what used to be Cuzzin's pick-up. Shea is with him. The truck now sports new signage:

Captain Artie, The Striper King
Tours and Lessons

Shea gets out with hand-held video recorder, and points it at Cuzzin. "Lights, camera, action," she says. "Guess who's making a promotional video about striped bass for the Massachusetts Harbor Association?"

"Don't look at me," says Cuzzin. "I just got out of the bait and tackle business."

"Me and my partner, The Captain. It's a history of the Harbor."

"As told from the perspective of a striped bass," says Artie. "I shit you not. And we've got a shooting budget of fifteen big ones. I used to be able to spend that much money on a cast party. Now, I've got to produce a thirty-minute film!"

"Fifteen grand," scoffs Cuzzin. "Pocket change."

"It's for a non-profit. Gives me an excuse to write off my fishing expenses."

Artie surveys the restaurant scene from the cab:

"Amazing what you can accomplish with a little elbow grease and a million bucks."

"Take the tour!" says Cuzzin. He's already developing the swagger of the impresario. The bait shop transformation is nearly complete. The kitchen is a study in stainless. The coolers and fryers stand at the ready. Workers move purposefully, bringing in supplies and making fine tunings adjustments. There's a clatter of purposefulness, chaos that's under control and moving towards order.

"In less that a week," says Cuzzin, "I'll be holding that ceremonial first piece of sushi in my hand. It will be perfectly coated. The oil will be at exactly 350 degrees and squeaky clean, thanks to my Gordon Filtron®. I'll throw it in and listen to the grease. There will be peace, harmony, and order in the world. And best of all, if I completely screw up, the bank sticks it to you, Ah-tee."

Cuzzin is so amused by his own humor that it sounds as if a motorcycle convention is being held in the parking lot. Elaine laughs and Cuzzin says, "What do you think is so funny, you frizzy-headed, smelly Jewish bitch?" She responds by saying his belly looks so fat because his head is shoved so far up his ass that it pushing out the front. Artie notices that Elaine's laugh is getting a little gravelly, too.

Artie's cell phone rings. He looks at the display to see who it is. "It's Spielberg," he announces.

Hey, Stephen. Howyadoin'? Yeah, we're still on. The absolute best time for you to come will be the third weekend in May. The highest tides of the spring. We're talking the weekend of the 18th. Does that work? Perfect.

You'll stay with me at the cottage, won't you? It might be a little cold. Bring a bottle of single malt. Don't worry about the equipment. I've got it covered. I'm going to put you right on top of some striped bass. I promise you.

Yeah, we can talk. OK, see ya.

"He's a nice man, and I'm not just saying that because he paid through the nose for the right to make the sequel to '*My Mother, My Lover...*' We'll bring him up here for some fried sushi, or maybe cook up lobsters at the cottage. After all, he did make all this possible." Artie gestures to the surrounding splendor of Cuzzin's Seafood.

"Yizz might say yowah the one who made this possible," says Cuzzin.

"Right," agrees Artie, "Or maybe we should thank this old babe who got Spielberg to pay millions more than what it was worth."

He pauses to take in Elaine, and puts his arm around her. "You have really become quite a rig. Didn't you used to be somebody?"

"You've got me mixed up with Arthur Gordon, who used to be a famous movie producer/director. Now he spends his time driving around in an old truck taking pictures of fish." Elaine may be wrapped in a different package, but her voice still hovers on the edge of aggression and whine. "So, Captain, how's business shaping up for the summer?"

"Spielberg in May. Bob Redford is coming out to do the Hasty Pudding thing at Harvard in June, and I'll be taking him out. And if the Lakers and Celtics-fat chance-hook up in the playoffs, then Jack will be out for a few days. He wants to stay at the cottage. And Bobby DeNiro also wants me to call him for the strongest spring tides, but that's when Spielberg is here. Liam's coming in a few weeks, and Joe Liquordup says they're going to occupy Faneuil Hall in August. He'll arrange the date around the best tides. So I'm booked solid, or as solid as I want to be."

They all look skyward to admire the giant fish, still attached to the crane, but now settled into place. "We can't stay long," says Shea. "We just heard that the first herring have arrived at the Weir River dam, and we need to get some footage for the documentary."

Artie takes another look at the transformed Elaine. "You know, when you hooked up with my cousin, somehow I thought you would get him to clean up his act. But you've descended right down to his level."

She fidgets, then quickly flips him the bird and suggests that he can kiss her flabby ass.

"I rest my case," says Artie. He continues his level gaze.

"So whaddya got? A staring problem?" she asks.

Artie shakes his head with a grin. "No, but I can't believe that I'm here and you're here with me. Did we really take the money and run?"

"Naw," she says, pulling at her nose and looking up at the fish, now settling into its final resting position on the roof, "That only happens in the movies. Hey, jizzwanna beer?"

The End

Stephen Hunter Morris writes about salt water, green mountains, wild turkeys, cluster flies, and, of course, Spam, the semi-edible kind. His previous novels include *Beyond Yonder* (Viking/Penguin) and *The King of Vermont* (William Morrow). His essays appear regularly in *The Vermont Sunday Magazine* and *Livin': The Vermont Way*. He is one of the founders of The Public Press. He lives in a part of Central Vermont that is next to nothing but close to everything, called Beyonder.

We are The Public Press. You are The Public Press.

Corporate media conglomerates continue to consume independents. While ownership consolidates, new book titles, specialized cable channels, and new websites proliferate. Amidst a din of commercial noise the bandwidth and coherence of available information is narrowing. Thoughtful authors find it more difficult to find publishers for sustained, original, and independent ideas at a time when technology is making it easier than ever to disseminate information.

The casualty is free speech.

The Public Press was founded in 2004 to protect freedom of speech "word-by-word." It is a grassroots organization, beholden only to its readers, its authors, and its partners.

These are the goals of The Public Press:

Empower authors. The Public Press puts the fewest possible filters or impediments between the creator and audience. The Public does not control the publishing process in the same way that a commercial publisher does. As a result there are stylistic and quality variations from title to title. The resulting books are like hearth-baked bread or handcrafted beer compared to more uniform, but less distinctive, products of commercial counterparts.